HERO'S RISK

TENNESSEE THUNDERBOLTS
BOOK 5

GINA AZZI

THREE CITIES PUBLISHING LLC

ONE
BEAU

"A REAL HOLLYWOOD STAR! In our town," a teenage girl gushes into her cell phone.

I fight the urge to roll my eyes as I pass through the hockey arena, The Honeycomb, toward the parking lot. The arena is busy today, brimming with adolescents and teenagers for a handful of clinics. Thank God this is the last week.

"She's from here, you know," another voice, a middle-aged woman in line at the cupcake stand, Primrose Sweets, says to her friend. "She graduated from Fallsview High."

"Class of 2013," the friend confirms.

My stomach sours at the name of my high school. And twists harder at the name of my ex-girlfriend.

Not just ex-girlfriend. The ex-love of my life. The one who got away...and stayed away. Until now.

The September heat hits me full-on as I push through the arena doors. My hockey team, the Tennessee Thunderbolts, have our season opener in two weeks. While the team is fixated on the season, my head is all over the place. Because last weekend, while my little sister Bea showed me the space she's renting to open her pottery store, she dropped a bomb in my lap.

Celine is coming home, to Knoxville, to film a movie.

Then, the bomb detonated.

Celine is arriving this week.

The news brought a fresh wave of anxiety.

Since my honorable discharge from the Marines over two years ago, I've had a rough time readjusting to civilian life. Of moving forward. Sure, I achieved my childhood dream of playing in the NHL, but hockey is the only thing that keeps me sane.

Off the ice, I feel the full weight of my deployments and duty tours. Anxiety wraps around my shoulders like a cloak, pulling tight when my control slips. When my routine is thrown off. When I doubt myself.

I thought I was getting better. When Bea moved home in January and took over Gran's care, it offered me the opportunity to move into my own space in Downtown Knoxville. Things, like breathing, started feeling easier. I was making progress.

Until now.

With Celine's impending arrival, it feels like I'm stuck in a straightjacket. My nerves are rattled, my control nonexistent, my insecurities on high alert. The woman who literally and figuratively brought me to my knees is back, living in our hometown, where our paths will undoubtedly cross. Regularly.

I toss my practice bag into the back seat of my truck and slide behind the steering wheel. I flip the ignition, blast the air conditioner, and drop my head to the headrest. Close my eyes. Breathe.

Celine and I saw each other at my gran's ninetieth birthday party in April. It was during that event that I learned Bea and Celine never lost touch, the same way Celine and I did. It was that celebration where I saw my ex-girl interact with my brothers like it was normal. Her love and concern for them overshadowing the awkwardness that exists between me and her.

Celine Hernandez, with her long, dark hair, her big, bedroom eyes, her luscious lips, is a mega movie star. But that weekend, she was still the bright-eyed beauty who climbed through my bedroom window every night the month after my parents passed. At fourteen, my world was ripped apart when the helicopter they were traveling in went down. Hell-bent on keeping my siblings safe and together as Gran navigated becoming our guardian overnight, Celine was my ride or die.

She taught Bea how to apply makeup. She made cupcakes for Brody's birthday party. She didn't flip out when Bodhi got his first neck tattoo. She was the steady, the calm, the rock of my whole fucking world.

Until she moved to LA and never looked back.

Fuck. I open my eyes and slap the steering wheel.

What the hell is she doing here? Why did she agree to this movie? Why does she want to plunge us back into the pain and heartache I've spent the past eight years trying to accept?

Pulling out of the arena, I point my truck in the direction of Gran's house. To cut the noise in my head, I flip on the radio.

"Celine Hernandez is coming back to town!" the host announces.

I turn it off.

Celine is everywhere, much as she was when we were younger. To think, I had to go all the way to Afghanistan to escape her presence and even there, her soulful eyes followed me into restless sleep.

She's the one that got away. The one I'll never win back.

There's too much hurt, too much resentment, on both of our sides to allow for it.

So, what the hell is she playing at?

"OF COURSE you'll stay for dinner," Gran talks over me as I think of an excuse to skip dinner tonight.

"Gran—"

"You need to eat better, Beau. You're an *athlete*," she emphasizes the word, like I somehow forgot that at twenty-eight, I'm living my dream career as an NHL player.

Bea laughs. "Listen to your grandmother, Beau."

Cole, my teammate and my little sister's boyfriend, passes me a glass of water. "You may as well give in," he advises.

I mumble under my breath but move back into the kitchen.

"Bodhi is coming to visit in a few weekends," Gran says, tossing me a smile. "I'll expect you that weekend, too."

I snort. "You say it as if I'm not here all the time."

"Sometimes when you're here, you're not really *here*," Gran shoots back.

Bea winces and Cole averts his gaze. My sister and her man relocate to the porch, leaving me with the dainty old lady who could best me at whatever she sets her mind to.

"Gran," I say gently.

"I know you carry demons, Beau." She turns, pointing her tongs at me. "But you've been back for two years now. It's time to start embracing civilian life. *Real* life."

"I am." I sound too defensive to be believable. I toss a hand in the air. "I have a job, an apartment, *friends*."

"No hobbies," Gran points out.

"I play—"

"It's your career," she cuts me off before I can utter the word *hockey*. "No girlfriends."

"I da—"

"Who?" She jumps in again, before "date" can leave my lips.

I roll the tension from my neck, reaching for calmness. Gran's words struck a nerve. But what does she want me to say? That I'm lonely? That my head still resides overseas half the time? That Celine still infiltrates my dreams?

"I worry about you, Beau." Her words are soft.

I find Gran's gaze. The genuine compassion in her slate blue eyes, the same shade as mine, centers me. "I'm okay, Gran."

Her mouth curves into an almost-smile. "Some days."

I heave out a sigh. "I'll stay for dinner."

This time, she gives me a real smile. "I'd like that very much."

"Okay." I move toward the porch so I can catch up with Bea.

"Set an extra place for yourself at the table," Gran calls after me.

I let out a chuckle. Pulling a plate and utensils from the cabinet, I head to the table, frowning when I count the place settings. I place down the extra items I pulled. "Gran, it's already set for four."

"I know," she says, cryptically, waving her cell phone at me. Blake just sent her the newest iPhone and she loves having the latest technology, even before Bea. "I have to take this, Beau. It's my doctor."

I wave her off, wondering who else is coming to dinner.

The screen door to the porch bangs closed and I hear my sister and Cole laughing, their voices hushed, as they move onto the porch and down the steps. They're probably taking a little walk, wanting to have time to themselves. Knowing they both navigate busy schedules keeps my feet rooted in the dining room. I don't want to interrupt them.

Years ago, when Celine and I were an us, I wonder if my siblings felt the same way. Did they think they were intruding when they caught us in an embrace? When they interrupted our laughter from an inside joke?

Probably not, considering my siblings were adolescents then. They didn't have the self-awareness to know what it felt like to be caught up in a woman, in a relationship, so intense, it rivaled gravity.

But having that experience, and losing it, makes Bea's breathless laughter and Cole's rumbling chuckle land differently. God, what is wrong with me that my sister's happiness —happiness she truly deserves—fills me with shadows of grief? With phantom pains of joy I haven't experienced in years?

Blowing out a deep breath, I pull the small pill bottle from my pocket and toss back a white tablet. The medication kicks in quickly, relieving some of the uncertainty that wars in my mind, easing some of the tension that knots the muscles in my neck.

Since my last deployment in Afghanistan, I've been on the anxiety medication. Slowly, my dosage has decreased, and my goal is to be completely off it in another year. But since the Celine Hernandez news landed in my lap like a grenade, I've needed the tablets to soften the edge.

The doorbell rings and I frown.

"Beau, can you get that?" Gran hollers.

I blow out another exhale and move toward the front door. Through the screen, I can make out the shape of a woman, her face blocked by the setting sun.

Then, I turn the corner, she comes into view, and my heart straight up stops.

Her smile, like warm honey, rolls over her face. She lifts a hand in greeting.

I yank open the door.

"Hi, Beau," Celine murmurs.

My eyes narrow, my heart rate ticks up. My fucking anti-anxiety meds feel useless in this moment that I am wholly unprepared for. "What are you doing here?"

Celine's smile slips. Her eyes dim. "You didn't know?"

I let out a humorless laugh. "About the movie? Yeah, it's all anyone can talk about."

She swallows, takes a second to collect her thoughts. She's not rash like the new me; Celine doesn't lose control. "No, I mean, about dinner. Gran invited me."

My laughter rings out again. Harsher this time.

My ex-everything flinches.

Guilt colors my shortcomings, making me feel worse, yet validated. "Of course she did," I bite out before I can stop myself.

Is this what Gran meant about dating?

Celine shuffles from one foot to the other, looking more uncomfortable, more out of place, than she ever has on this porch before. "I brought dessert." She thrusts a box from Annabelle's bakery, presumably a buttermilk pie, in my direction.

I sigh, knowing how long the wait for one of Annabelle's pies can be. Hours. It's a thoughtful gesture and—wait, did Celine send an assistant to collect the pie? When did she get into town? I thought she wasn't coming for a few more days. Why didn't Gran tell me? Surely, Bea would have prepared me for this meeting, this dinner.

Celine clears her throat delicately. "Can I come in?"

I blink slowly, trying to eradicate the random thoughts from my mind. This isn't an ambush, it's dinner at my gran's house. I dig deep and find my manners. "Of course." I step aside and hold the screen door as Celine slips inside.

"Celine!" My sister reappears, rushing up the steps and into the house. She wraps my ex in a hug.

"Oh, Bea! I'm so happy to be home," Celine shares.

Over their embrace, Cole meets my eyes. Whatever he reads in mine causes a tick to pop in his jaw. But in the next moment, it's gone as he kisses Celine's cheek in greeting.

Gran appears, ushering Celine into her home. She peppers her with questions about her film, her flight, her life in LA.

I fall into step behind my family, following them into the dining room as Gran pulls out a chair for Celine. Bea fills her wine glass. Cole steps in to take the pie from my hands.

He lets out a low whistle. "Annabelle's. She's not playing."

"No," I agree, clearing my throat.

Celine Hernandez isn't one for games. She's a straight shooter, aims right for the fucking heart. I learned that the hard way.

Now that she's back, I can't forget it.

Just like I can't forget her.

TWO
CELINE

"YOUR CHICKEN POT pie is what dreams are made of," I tell Gran, helping myself to a second serving. My trainer will bitch at me in the morning but right now, I don't care.

Sitting in Gran's dining room, surrounded by the cinnamon and potpourri scent, eating a warm meal, fills me with nostalgia. I was here in April to celebrate Gran's nineti-eth, but it was a busy day, and the house was filled with friends and family.

Right now, it's quiet, peaceful, simple. Reliable. Just the way I remember.

Beau makes a sound in his throat, and I look up. It's a tampered down sound of amusement except it's at odds with his narrowed, sharp eyes. I narrow mine back, waiting for him to expand.

"Gran's pot pie? Celine, you eat at fancy, Michelin-starred restaurants in LA," he reminds me as if I've forgotten. As if I haven't worked my ass off to eat at those restaurants, only to realize that some things, most things, taste sweeter when shared with the people you love.

Clearly, it's a lesson I learned too late.

Instead of responding, I take another bite of chicken pot pie. Bea ducks her head, while Cole, her hockey playing boyfriend, shoots Beau a warning look. Gran, with zero fucks to give, smacks her grandson in the back of his head.

"Ow," he winces.

"That's all you have to say?" Gran asks, her voice stern. Another thing I remember. I start to smile.

Beau looks right at me, and my smile dies on my lips. Because he's looking at me like he can't stand me. Like he hates that I'm sitting here, in his family's house, when it used to feel like my home too.

"Excuse me, Celine," Beau says by way of apology.

I drop my chin in acceptance. He scrapes the last bite of food from his place and grabs it, moving to shove back from the table.

Tension radiates off Beau's shoulders. He doesn't want me here; he doesn't like seeing me in his space. Is it because the past is painful for him to remember too? Or is it because he doesn't want me as part of his present? Maybe both. The thought saddens me.

Even with his rigid posture and standoffish body language, he looks good. Scratch that; he looks amazing. Infinite fire emojis. His shoulders, packed with anger he'd like to hurl my way, are broad, his biceps stretching the material of his T-shirt. After years in the military, followed by hockey training, Beau Turner is in the best shape of his life.

While his body is rocking, his energy unsettles me. The boyish tilt of his smirk has hardened into a manly scowl. The bright amusement of his slate blue eyes has dimmed into a haunted darkness. Beau grew up but he also changed in ways I'll never understand. Not counting our seeing each other at Gran's party, we haven't spoken since that ill-fated day he surprised me in LA.

It was the day I got my big break. Professionally, it was my unicorn day.

Personally, it was the day I broke my own heart. Although, I didn't know it at the time. I didn't fully realize it until years later, until moments like now. When the nostalgia of my teenage years wraps around me like English Ivy, and I don't know if I should sink into its hold or try to break free.

Beau stills as Gran tightens her hold. When she's sure he's not going to bolt, she resumes eating.

"How long will filming take?" Cole, thoughtful and empathetic, asks to redirect the attention.

Bea gives him a grateful smile and I take a moment to drink in the sweet first love before me. Bea is like a little sister to me and witnessing her happiness, with a great guy, fills my cup.

"Three to four months. I'm anticipating staying until the end of the year," I say.

"Is it weird to be back?" Cole asks again.

"Kind of," I admit, laughing. I place my fork down and lean back in my chair, taking my wine glass with me. I take a long sip. "It's nostalgic. In many ways, it seems like my entire life is different now but coming home, it still feels the same."

"Yeah, not much has changed here," Beau mutters.

Cole and Bea ignore him.

"Where are you staying?" Bea asks.

At this, Beau's eyes snap to mine. I feel his stare on my profile, but I don't give him the satisfaction of meeting his gaze.

Beau scoffs. "You can tell us if you've got the penthouse at the Premier Hotel or something. We're not going to judge you. Well, not *too* much."

Gran sighs.

I smirk. "Actually, I'm staying off Hartzel Lane."

Bea's eyebrows furrow. "In the woods?"

"Basically." I laugh again. "It's so quiet there. It's—"

"In the middle of nowhere," Beau chimes in again, his jaw

tight. "What property did you rent? There aren't many. Why aren't you staying with your parents if you're not at a hotel?"

"Mom and Dad relocated a few years ago," I respond, wondering how he didn't know that. The realization that he's tried so hard to block out all mention of me, he didn't even know my family left Tennessee, cuts. It shouldn't, but it does.

Surprise ripples over Beau's expression and it's satisfying, knowing I surprised him on some level. "To where?"

"California. Pasadena, so not far from me."

"And Marisa and Louis?" He asks about my siblings.

"Marisa is at university, in Texas. Louis is expecting a baby." I smile when I say it. I can't wait to be an aunt. "He and his wife are in Oregon."

Beau shakes his head, as if shaking off his surprise. "So, no one is here anymore."

"Nope."

"And you still wanted to film a movie here?"

"I'm here, aren't I?" I toss back.

His mouth snaps shut, and he averts his gaze, apparently not liking my sass. That's okay; I don't appreciate his attitude either.

"Is the place you're staying...okay?" Cole asks tentatively, bringing the conversation around. "It's secure?"

I wave a hand. "Yeah, it's good. I haven't had much time there yet. I dropped my bags and came here for dinner."

Beau's eyes narrow again. "You just flew in today?"

I nod.

"What property is it?" he asks again.

"The Klingers' old place. You remember it?"

Beau's expression is carefully neutral. A long time ago, a bunch of kids from our graduating class had a bonfire by the Klingers' old place. Beau and I hooked up in their barn. "The Klingers' old place..."

"It's so peaceful out there," Bea sighs dreamily.

"It really is. I thought it'd be nice to have the change of scenery, the change of pace. Quiet coffee mornings with chirping birds," I explain.

Beau heaves out a sigh, as if he's single-handedly keeping humanity alive. "It's in the middle of nowhere. What if you have paparazzi or stalkers hounding you for autographs or photos or whatever?"

I arch an eyebrow, surprised that *that's* his first thought. But then again, it's in his nature to be cautious, to worry. "My security detail starts on Monday."

"And until then?" Beau asks.

I grin. "I think I'll be okay for a few days. It's home, after all." I tip my head toward Bea. "I may even go wild and buy a car while I'm here. My first one," I add, the anticipation filling me with a bubble of giddiness. I've waited a long time to buy my own car. It's not that I haven't owned vehicles before. I bought Mom and Dad new cars years ago and have been gifted a few cars over the years as well.

But I've never entered a dealership and purchased a car to drive myself around in. In LA, I have a driver. The past few years, I've hardly been there as I've been on set, mostly in Estonia, filming the fantasy series *Midnight Moon* that made my career.

Right now, I have a driver on standby. Depending on what my security team decides next week, this may be my chance to drive myself around like a regular person.

Cole shakes his head ruefully. "You got a license?"

"Yes!" I tap the table. "But I haven't driven myself around in years. I'm looking forward to the…normalcy of it all."

"Most of us would take the driver," Beau quips.

I ignore him.

"How'd you get here tonight?" he asks after a beat.

I roll my eyes. "Driver."

Gran cackles.

I grin back, so happy to be in her home.

She reaches for my hand and squeezes it.

I squeeze back, grateful. "It's good to be home, Gran."

"It's good to have you here, my dear."

At the end of a long day, I wanted a refuge, a slice of normal that's been lacking in my life for too damn long. I want...home. That's why I'm renting the Klingers' place, away from the pull of Knoxville, away from the noise and the cameras and the swarms of people.

I want a slice of peace; instead, I've got Beau Turner glaring at me like I ate the last slice of Annabelle's buttermilk pie.

Bea and Cole stand and begin to clear away our dinner plates. I hop up to help but Gran's hand on my arm stops me.

"I'll be back with the pie and coffee," she says pointedly.

I sit back down as Gran follows Bea and Cole into the kitchen.

When it's just Beau and me in the dining room, Beau leans back in his chair. He interlaces his fingers, his hands folded on top of the table. He watches me intently. "You don't feel at home in LA?"

I blow out a sigh, wondering what his angle is with this line of questioning. What does he want me to say? That I'm lonely, that I still think of him, that I regret not investing in our relationship the way he did when I had the chance?

"What are you doing here, Celine? Why'd you come back?"

His words punch through me like a physical blow. I drain my wine glass.

"I could be nominated for an Oscar for this performance," I say softly.

Disappointment colors his eyes and I know it was the wrong thing to say. My stomach knots, guilt and pressure and frustration with myself flaring.

"So, it's just about the work," Beau comments.

I arch an eyebrow. "You want it to be about something else?"

He glares at me, his mouth twisting into a frown. I wait him out, silently hoping he gives me something—but what?—to work with. Beau clears his throat. "Not even a little," he says with a finality that cuts through my thin tough-girl bravado.

I drop my head, studying the embroidered tablecloth.

"Things are different now," he adds, not unkindly.

I nod.

"Here comes pie!" Bea announces, balancing several small dishes. She places a slice down in front of me. "Thanks for bringing this. It's my favorite."

I force a smile; my cheeks ache. "I know." I pick up my fork and take a bite, my eyes dropping closed as the delicious, decadent taste—of Sunday mornings of my childhood, with Dad reading the newspaper and Mom making coffee—rolls through me.

Gran appears with the coffee.

"Thank you, Gran."

"You know, you're welcome to stay here," she offers. "I'd love a roommate."

"Hey!" Bea waves her hand. "You got me."

"Pfft." Gran flicks a dismissive hand. Her eyes dart between Bea and Cole. "You're a woman of the night; we all know it."

Bea blushes, her cheeks and neck turning a bright red color. Cole bites into an apple, the loud crunch like a fire-cracker in the silent dining room. Beau swears.

Gran smacks the back of his head. "Not at the table."

"Sorry, Gran," he murmurs.

I snort out a laugh, smiling at her since I know her offer is sincere. It warms me from the inside out that Gran still holds me in high regard even though things between Beau and me didn't work out. "Thanks, Gran. But I'm looking forward to spending some time here on my own. To just *be*."

Gran studies me for a long moment before patting my hand in acceptance.

"If you need anything," Cole starts, "I live close by and I'm pretty handy. I could—"

"I'll take you home and check out your place," Beau cuts him off.

Bea hides her grin behind a gulp of coffee.

Gran nods approvingly. "He finally comes to his senses," she murmurs.

"That's not necessary," I say. "I can call—"

"Oh, don't make your driver come back out all this way," Gran cuts me off. "Beau's gotta pass right by the Klingers' place on his way home."

"Exactly," Beau agrees, his eyes flashing to mine, as if it's settled. Then, in a lower tone, "At least let me check it out, Celine. Make sure you're safe."

It's hard to argue with that. Beau always was a protector. He brought up his younger siblings after his parents' death, he served in the Marines, he always puts the safety and well-being of others above everything else.

The fact that that hasn't changed makes me breathe out a little sigh of relief.

"Okay," I agree. "Thank you, Beau."

"Don't thank him yet." Gran pats my hand. "Cole is handier. And much more pleasant company."

Bea giggles.

Cole winks. "You trying to butter me up so I'll sign up for another dance class?"

"Is it working?" Gran asks.

I sputter out a laugh, missing this family. Missing the broody man sitting across from me who looks like he can't stand me one minute and would drop everything to help me the next.

But just because Beau is a protector by nature doesn't mean he still harbors feelings for me. His offering me a ride should be taken at face value. If the past few years without him have taught me anything, it's that he can certainly hold a grudge.

By the steel edge ringing his irises, that's not going to change any time soon. And it's best I remember it.

THREE
BEAU

MY CONCERN EASES as I pull to a stop in front of Celine's rental. I haven't been out this way in ages, and I note the renovations that have taken place in the past few years.

A simple two-bedroom bungalow, with white shiplap siding and large, barn beams holding up the front porch, sits before us. "It looks nice," I admit.

Celine flashes me one of her heartbreaker smiles. I feel it like a punch to the gut. God, she's beautiful. Still as intoxicating as the first time I kissed her when I was twelve and she was eleven.

I blow out a deep breath. I need to get my thoughts under control.

I flip the ignition on my truck and Celine's head swivels in my direction. Her chocolate brown eyes are nearly black. Mysterious eyes I used to willingly lose myself in. Now, I'd never survive the drowning. "You don't have to come in."

I open the driver's side door in response.

Beside me, Celine huffs and the sound—cute and frustrated—almost makes me smile. We walk to her small house, surrounded by acres of heavily wooded property, slowly. We're both lost in our thoughts. The sun is setting, the sky a cotton candy swirl; the heat is bearable, with a whispering breeze stirring around us.

The scenery, the time of day, the scent of Celine's perfume —Valentino, the same one her mom always wore—serves as a throwback. We're not Beau and Celine, two strangers with a shared history and a list of regrets. For a handful of heartbeats, we're Beau and Celine, two teenagers so desperately in love, every touch lingers, every kiss promises, and every day ahead seems certain, rooted in *knowing*.

"Watch your step," Celine warns, pointing to the small top step that serves as a lip to the porch.

I dip my head in thanks.

"Your parents coming out for a visit?" I ask.

"For Christmas," she beams. "Can you imagine? All of us back here again. I'm hosting."

I can't fight the smile that forms on my face. She seems genuinely happy to be here, back in our small town that she was once desperate to escape. I didn't expect it; I didn't expect her to be…the way I remember. "That's good."

"Yeah," she agrees, unlocking the front door.

I step inside after her, closing and locking the door.

"I literally dropped my bags and went to Gran's, so I haven't had much time to look around. But everything checks out," she assures me as I check the lock on her front door before moving to the windows in the living room.

"Your kitchen faucet is leaking," I inform her.

She gasps, clutching her heart. "My kitchen faucet?" She drapes the back of her hand over her forehead. "How will I survive the danger?"

"Cute," I comment, pointing at her. "You should be an actress."

She laughs, the sound beautiful. Her face while she does it, mesmerizing. I pause and take it in—the crinkles around her eyes, the gleam of her teeth, and elegant column of her throat—God, did I fucking love this woman. Listening to her laughter eases some of the tightness that permanently lives in my chest. I let out a long exhale and wish we were those naive, drunk-love, teenagers again. If only for a night.

I move onto the back sliding door that steps out onto a little deck with two Adirondack chairs. When the lock doesn't latch, I swear. "Lock's broken."

At this, Celine's laughter fades. Worry washes over her expression. "Seriously?"

"Yeah," I peer at her. "I'll be right back."

"Where are you going?" she calls after me as I move through her house and out the front door.

I don't bother responding. Instead, I pull a toolbox from the bed of my truck.

Celine's laughter wafts over me as I move up her porch. "You still carry around a toolbox?"

"Don't know when you'll need it," I reply, entering her home and heading to the sliding door.

I force myself to turn away from her to inspect the broken lock. I dig around my toolbox and come up with a temporary solution. "This will be okay for tonight, but I'll pass by tomorrow with a stronger lock." I glance at her over my shoulder. "You have any issues with stalkers? Paparazzi?" It's the second time I've brought it up and it's something I know she deals with, if only from the number of times her face has been printed on the front of one of the gossip magazines in the supermarket check-out aisles.

"Not at the moment," she says. "Paparazzi love me."

I frown. "I'm being serious."

"So am I," she says, her eyes thoughtful. "But I am cautious. That's why my security team starts Monday."

"Yeah," I grunt. "You can always take Gran up on her offer," I toss out. "Even if only for the weekend."

The thought of her needing a security team, of needing their presence to secure her safety, unsettles me. It makes the tightness in my chest tug, like a band of pressure.

Images, unbidden and fucking awful, roll through my mind.

Women, children, villages pillaged and burned. Rape. Violence. Devastation. My stomach churns and the taste of bile, repugnant, coats the back of my throat.

I force myself to study the lock, to pick up a screwdriver. I focus on my breathing to slow my racing heart. I try to think of anything other than the debilitating images hijacking my mind.

My fingers tremble and I drop the screw I'm holding. "Shit," I mutter, reaching for it.

Celine picks it up before me. She holds it out, her dark eyes brimming with curiosity. Questions and compassion I don't want to answer and don't deserve. I swipe it from her hand and shove it into the makeshift lock.

"I don't want to put Gran out," she says finally.

"It's no trouble," I say around the end of the second screw pinched between my teeth.

"I'll be fine for the weekend, Beau. You know this area is perfectly safe." Celine's hand lands in the center of my back and my body locks down from her touch. Her palm presses into my skin, comforting, anchoring, and ripping old wounds wide open. All at the same damn time.

My skin feels too tight, my muscles coiled and ready to spring, my heart battering against my rib cage.

I open my mouth and a gunshot rings out. Loud and too fucking close.

"Get down!" I yell, pivoting on my back foot and lunging at Celine.

Shock registers on her expression before I wrap her in my arms and cover her body with mine, keeping her pinned to the floor.

Another shot rings out and my head swims. It's a hunting rifle. The thought ricochets around my mind—a logical voice of reason. But other images leap to the forefront—RPGs and rapid gunfire, laser lights and smoke. I feel disoriented, my mind ripped in two. My hands are shaking, my frantic heartbeat pressing into Celine's chest, letting her know just how rattled I am. I look around her place, seeing that there's no danger even though it *feels* imminent.

"Beau, Beau!" Celine calls my name, over and over.

I look down at her and her hands plant against my chest, shoving me back. I go easily, horror dawning as I realize that I just tackled her. Pinned her to the fucking floor. "Fuck. Oh shit." I reach for her, but she scoots back on her ass, her expression wary.

And it rips my heart out of my chest because my girl—the only one that ever mattered—is scared of me.

"I'm so sorry. I…shit." I pinch the bridge of my nose, willing my vision to clear. I shake my head, as if that will shake out the terrifying images, the bad thoughts, the constant sense of foreboding, all in one go.

"Beau…what…I…are you okay?" Celine asks. She cradles one wrist against her chest and my guilt detonates in my stomach like an IED.

"I hurt you," I say the words aloud. I move toward her slowly, cautiously, like she's a skittish animal about to flee when that more aptly describes me.

I reach for her again and this time, she lets me take her wrist.

"It's fine," she murmurs. "I just landed weird."

I touch the skin gently, prodding to check for injury. "It might be sprained."

She works a swallow. "I'll ice it."

I nod, still holding on to her hand. "Celine—"

"It's okay."

"It's not." I shake my head.

"Was…" She pauses, and my eyes cut to hers, wanting her to finish her question. Wanting to know every single thought swimming in her head. Does she hate me? Is she scared of me? Does she think I'm weak? Incapable of protecting her the way I once could? "Was Afghanistan that bad?" She winces, rolls her eyes. "I mean, I know it was. But did you see a lot of combat?"

Slowly, I nod, the images and sounds, bursts of color, flashes of noise, still loud in my head. I work a swallow, hating that she correctly read my reaction. Partly, I want to shield her, protect everyone I care about, from the things that keep me up at night. And partly, I hate that I'm so transparent. Why haven't I locked this shit down yet? Why can't I get a handle on it? "It was unimaginable," I admit, my voice cracking. Fuck, I hate how shaky I sound, like I'm about to pass out. "And I can't unsee any of it."

Celine's eyes hold mine, piercing me to my core. They're devoid of judgement, shadowed with concern more than anything. Concern for me when for years, I worried about her.

The realization is sobering. I blow out a breath, shaken and on edge. "I didn't mean to scare you."

"I'm okay," she reassures me.

I stand and reach for her uninjured hand, pulling her to her feet.

"Let me run and get you some ice," I say.

Celine shakes her head. "I've got groceries arriving soon." She pulls out her phone and taps the screen. "Ice packs, added."

I frown that she can be so flippant about this.

I literally just lost my cool in front of her.

I need to get out of here. I need to…what?

Rein it in, Turner. Bury this shit.

But can I really leave her?

"I'll be back tomorrow with a stronger lock," I say, by way of explaining all the things I can't say.

Celine gives me a small smile. "Thanks for the ride, Beau."

She begins walking to her front door and I fall into step beside her.

"Do you need anything?"

"I'm all set. Thanks"—her gaze drifts to the sliding door—"for fixing the lock."

"And tackling you in the process?" I snort out, beyond pissed off with myself for losing my cool like that.

Celine witnessing me that weak, that out of control, makes me feel like jumping out of my skin. Embarrassment sears me from the inside out.

She shakes her head, her hand resting on my bicep. I still, missing the feel of her touch. "It's okay, Beau. I'm really okay."

"Yeah," I agree noncommittally. "Give me your phone."

She frowns but hands over her phone.

I tap in my number, save it. I bite back my smile when I see that I'm still in her phone—just Beau, no last name—even though my number is old. Instead, I update it, liking that she kept me with her all these years.

I pass back the phone. "Now you have my new number."

"You changed it?"

"After the Marines."

"Oh, right," she says, pressing a button. In my back pocket, my cell buzzes. "Now you have mine too." She smiles.

"You need something, call."

"Will do."

I nod. "'Bye, Celine."

"See you, Beau."

I step outside, pull in a deep inhale, and walk back to my truck. I stow my toolbox in the back, lift a hand in farewell, and back out of the driveway.

It's surreal, having Celine back in town. Seeing her again, after all these years, kicks up a shit ton of complicated feelings.

That night, after tossing and turning for hours, they multiply. The turmoil I feel invades my dreams—shadows and flashes of light, agonized screams and terrified cries.

I wake around 4 AM, my T-shirt soaked through with sweat.

"Fuck," I mutter, wiping a palm over my face. I take an anxiety pill.

I pull myself from bed, change my sheets, and go for a long, sunrise run.

Then, I buy bagels and coffee and swing by Gran's.

She smiles when she pulls open her porch door.

"Got any sweet tea?" I ask.

"You bet. Sweetest in Tennessee." Gran holds open the door and I slip inside. She wraps an arm around my waist and lets me guide her into the kitchen.

She doesn't need my help, but she lets me have this. She lets me feel like I'm in control again, even though I haven't been in years.

Even though any semblance of it evaporated when Celine Hernandez rolled back into town.

FOUR
CELINE

"EVERYTHING'S FINE," I tell Charlie, my friend with some benefits, as I cradle my cell between my ear and shoulder.

"You sure you're settling in okay?" he asks, the concern evident in his tone.

I pull the orange juice from my refrigerator and pour a glass. Extra pulp, just the way I like it. "More than sure." I take a sip and smack my lips. "It feels good to be home. Normal."

Charlie chuckles through the line. "You say that like our lives aren't normal but, Cel, they are. They're just our *new* normal."

"Yeah," I mutter. For years, the life I'm living—high-profile actress, residing in LA, invited to exclusive events and parties, splashed across the covers of magazines—was my dream. Now, I'm in it and still, something is missing. I sigh. "This morning, still in my pajamas, I had coffee on my back porch, and just stared at the trees. I felt the sunshine on my face and listened to the birds and it was *better*, you know?"

"Better than…"

"The noise and the chaos and the constant worry of being

photographed," I rattle off the list of concerns that regularly plagues my mind in LA. Even though it's a life I busted my ass for, and I know I shouldn't complain because I'm fortunate to have made my career out of my passion, I miss normal. Crave it. "Everyone always…wanting something."

Charlie chuckles. "You say that now, babe. And I get it. You haven't had a holiday in a long time. It's nice to kick back and space out for a bit."

"Yeah," I say softly, spinning in the middle of my living room. I needed this time to myself more than I realized.

"But you'll miss LA. You'll come back. People like us always do."

People like us. Ambitious, driven, passionate. Charlie and I met on the first day of shooting *Midnight Moon*. That series was a breakout role for both of us. It's where we got our starts, together. The past seven years, filming, traveling, working together, has formed one of the strongest friendships of my life with one of the only actors I've ever truly been myself around.

Somewhere into the second season of our show, Charlie and I started hooking up. It was casual at first, then a little more intense. Charlie's expressed his feelings for me on more than one occasion but I've never been able to take that step with him. We may accompany each other to events or premieres but we aren't dating. We hook up from time to time but it's never exclusive. The media loves to report on our comings and goings but they're not what they seem. We're friendship with a side of attraction. While Charlie hopes it will develop into more, I don't think that will happen.

I think it even less now that I've seen Beau again. Even though Beau and I have no future together, I know that the feelings he evokes are stronger than the ones Charlie stirs. Is it always like that with a first love? Does it haunt you forever and force you to eventually settle?

The thought depresses me.

"Do those dates work?" Charlie's question brings me back to the conversation and I realize I checked out.

"Say that again?"

He snorts. "Those birds must be chirping loudly."

I laugh. "Sorry. What did you say?"

"I think I can come visit the first weekend in November. Do those dates work?"

"Um, sure?" I guess. "I haven't looked at the schedule yet."

Charlie sighs and I know, deep down, that he wishes I missed him as much as he misses me when we're both traveling for work and go months without hanging out. "Let me know when you get a chance, okay?"

"I will," I promise. Movement outside my front window catches my eye and I walk closer. My heart rate accelerates as Beau's navy-blue truck pulls into my driveway.

I roll my lips together to keep from smiling. He swings down from his truck, and I can't tear my eyes away.

Jeans mold to his perfect ass and strong thighs. He's rocking a blue plaid shirt, the sleeves rolled up on his forearms. He's dressed way too warmly for the weather, but he looks comfortable, wearing the same "uniform" I remember from high school.

Beau's never been fussy. While Charlie has more hair and skin care products than me, Beau's never applied moisturizer. At least, not when I knew him. The only thing that's noticeably changed from Beau Turner from high school to Beau Turner now are the shadows that haunt his eyes, the severity of his expression, and his ride. He upgraded. Other than that, he's the same cautious, salt-of-the-Earth, steadfast guy I couldn't help but fall in love with.

He grabs his trusty toolbox from the trunk and this time, I can't fight the grin. He also has a white plastic bag in hand as he approaches my porch.

"I gotta go, Charlie," I tell my friend, before saying good-bye and hanging up.

Moving to the front door, I pause at the small console with the mirror in the foyer. My hair is pulled back in a twist, but the front pieces have escaped, framing my face. I fluff up my roots, swipe my fingertips across my eyebrows, and pinch my cheeks for some color.

I'm not going to win any awards, but I look…like myself. The realization makes me smile just as a knock sounds on my door.

I pull it wide open and arch an eyebrow. "Miss me that much?"

Beau smirks and holds up the plastic bag. "I brought you an alarm system."

I snort and step back so he can enter the space. "You didn't have to do that."

"Wanted to," he mutters like that settles it. Beau toes off his sneakers and beelines to the back door, dropping to his knees to get to work.

"Want an orange juice?"

He glances up. "Extra pulp?"

My smile is back. "Obviously."

A small huff. "Yeah, sure."

I get him a glass. He fiddles with the lock.

And it feels *normal*.

For a heartbeat, standing in the clean, bright kitchen, holding a glass of OJ, I can envision the life we would have had if I didn't leave. If he didn't cut me off. If we had stayed and built things, together.

It would have been *this*. And this is cozy. Stable. Real.

He clicks his tongue in satisfaction as he tests the new lock, and it works.

"Here." I hand him the glass.

"Thanks." He takes a swig before taking out the alarm box.

I point my foot, my pink toenails flashing, in his direction. "This isn't necessary."

He gives me a look. "Humor me."

"But thanks for doing it."

Beau nods and opens the package.

I sit at the kitchen island and watch him install the device. He's efficient, scanning the directions as he hooks it up. His eyebrows bend together and sometimes, he mouths the words to himself as he carries out the action.

I enjoy watching him. Seeing him work, his hands steady, his mind focused. It's hard to believe that eight years have passed since we've spent any time alone together.

It's also hard to believe that we're behaving rationally and considerate toward one another when in April, Beau was straight-up pissed off that I attended Gran's ninetieth birthday celebration.

When Beau is finished, he cleans up the packaging, snaps his toolbox closed, and slips his hands into his back pockets. Rocking on his heels, he looks at me. "All set."

"Thank you, Beau. Really."

"It's no trouble." He stalls.

I slip from my barstool, my stomach rumbling. I glance at my ex. But before he was my ex, he was my friend. In many ways, he's always been my *person*. Could we be in each other's lives again? "Are you hungry?"

Beau's head tilts to the side as he studies me, his lips pressing together. "Celine—"

"Don't shoot down a casual lunch, Beau."

"Is it really casual?" he flips back.

I shrug. He sighs.

"Celine, I'm sorry about last night."

I frown, my eyebrows tugging together.

"How's your wrist?" he reminds me.

"I'm fine, Beau. You didn't have to do this"—I fling a hand toward my back door—"out of guilt."

"I didn't." He sounds defensive.

I lift my eyebrows.

"I did it because I worry about you. Always have."

I bite my bottom lip as a tremble runs through me. I clear my throat. "I'm a grown woman; I can take care of myself."

"I know you can. Doesn't mean I don't worry."

I stare at him for a long beat and feel the weight of his words move through me, slow as molasses, warm as whiskey. "Tacos?" I grin.

He snorts, his eyes flaring in disbelief. "You seriously want to hang out?"

"Sure."

"Don't you have, I don't know, read-throughs to go to? Or appointments to attend?"

"I'm off the clock until next week. Everyone's settling in town; I came early."

"Why?" His tone is curious.

I scrunch up my nose, glance out the back sliding door to the gorgeous scenery. "Missed it. Missed this."

"This?" His voice is lower than it was a moment ago and my stomach dips at the rasp in it.

I cut my eyes back to him. "This," I confirm, not expanding on what *this* means. Because I mean all of it. Home and him and here.

He's silent for a long minute. My heart thuds, worried he's going to shut me out. Then he drops one shoulder, clasps the back of his neck, and tugs. "I can run out and get tacos."

I wave a hand and reach for my phone. "I'll order."

Beau shakes his head. "No way. The less people who know where you live, the better."

I give him a look.

"What?" he asks.

"Didn't you hear? I have a fancy alarm system now."

Beau snorts. "I'll get the tacos," he repeats, taking my

phone from my hands. "Right after I show you how to set the alarm."

He downloads the necessary app, taps in a bunch of info, and shows me how to arm and disarm my new system.

"Thanks," I say when he passes me back the phone. I move toward my purse and pull out my wallet.

Beau's expression hardens. "Put your wallet away."

"It's for the alarm—"

"Put it away, Celine." He bends down to retrieve his toolbox and heads toward the front door. "I'll be back."

"Wait." I follow him out, knowing better than to argue with him about the money. He won't accept it. "Don't you want to know what I want?"

He glances at me over his shoulder, one foot already on the porch step. "Two beef tacos with extra hot sauce, no cheese. One fish taco with extra pico, no guac."

My steps halt as he rattles off my old order. "You remember?"

Beau's expression sobers, the playfulness in his eyes dimming. He holds my gaze, pins me right to the core. "I remember, Celine." It's as if he's talking about our entire relationship, our high highs and low lows, in those two words. He dips his head. "I'll be back."

"I'll be here," I quip.

He points at me. "Set the alarm."

I grin. "Yes, sir."

At my word choice, his mouth flattens again.

I shift from one foot to the other, feeling stupid for tossing that out. It's obvious that Beau is struggling from his time in the Marines. I hate the anguish that cut through his eyes last night. The fear that radiated off his body made me feel sick. The fact that he carries around those old feelings, day in and day out, causes my concern for him to spike.

Does anyone know that he's struggling? Is he talking to a professional? Or seeking out support?

Beau honks his horn twice before pulling out of the driveway. I watch him go, lift a hand in a wave, and slip back inside my place. I set the alarm.

Then, I look around the space and wish it was mine. Wish it was ours.

Wish, if just for a little while, that I picked a different path, that I chose the man, when I still had the chance.

FIVE
BEAU

I STALL after picking up the tacos. Drive around for ten minutes, with the windows down, the music thrumming in my veins, and try to get a handle on myself.

My head is fucked. It has been for years. But now it's screwed up in a different way. I'm not just fighting against the onslaught of images from my deployments; I'm fortifying myself for the assault of memories with Celine.

The good ones: Celine spinning around, her face upturned, her laughter wild, in a snowstorm in New York. The first time we had sex, the trust that burned in her eyes like a meteor shower, all light and sparkle. When my hockey team won a championship and my girl vaulted herself onto the ice and into my arms. My team cheered, my coaches smacked me on the back but laughed. We were crazy in love, caught up and sometimes, I wish I knew to savor the sweet longer. I wish I knew it wouldn't last so the devastation that came afterwards wouldn't have wrecked me.

But then, that devastation came. And I also carry around the bad: Celine's up and moving to LA, her mouth set in defiance. Celine's ultimatum: move with me or this isn't going to work. The day I surprised her in LA, my mom's engagement ring burning a hole in the pocket of my jeans, only to have her take a phone call during dinner and run into her bedroom, shouting and laughing, as she pulled out a suitcase and began to pack for the opportunity that changed her career.

For the adventure of a lifetime, she said.

And she did it without me. Without even *thinking* about me.

I release a heavy exhale and turn my truck in the direction of her place. I know I have to let things go; I need to move on. But move on to what? It's a silly notion when everything I've ever wanted is shimmying around the living room of a cozy, farmhouse-style bungalow, rolling her eyes at my antics.

I park in front of her house and grip the takeout bag. Before I ascend the porch steps, Celine's standing in the doorway. "Those smell delicious."

"They're not Tacos and Tequila, but they're pretty good." I enter her home.

She shuts the door after me, shaking her head. "Remember Tacos and Tequila?" A dreamy expression crosses her face, as if she's remembering it the same way I am.

But that's impossible. Because when I remember the little taco eatery that closed two years after I left Tennessee, all I remember is Celine. Her hair was longer then, down to her ass. It was pin straight but curled just at the ends, just above the sweet dimples in her lower back. She used to wear a ball cap when we went in there, joking that her father would disown her for eating there when he frequented Alberto's Taqueria. It was a long running joke, but Mr. Hernandez knew we went there all the time.

I turn away from her, desperate to clear my mind, and place the takeout bag on the kitchen island. Celine's already set the table for us and it's a sweet gesture. A pang cuts through my chest as I sit, wishing this was real.

Wishing it *could* be real. But that's a joke because the ship for Celine and I didn't just sail away. It sank in the middle of the Atlantic during a hurricane.

Celine pours us sweet tea and gives me a look. "Don't start with me because it's not Gran's."

I snort. "It's okay; no one's is."

I open our takeout and place Celine's tacos on her plate. She sits next to me and digs in, her first moan of appreciation making my throat dry and my stomach clench.

I look at her and smile. Her eyes are closed and she's eating with gusto, even though the sounds falling from her mouth are indecent. "When's the last time you had a taco?"

She holds her taco higher, staring at it. "Way too long."

I shake my head and pick up my first taco.

For a few moments, we eat in silence and it's nice. Not riddled with tension, absent from expectations, just two people with a complicated history enjoying a meal together.

"It was nice to see your family, everyone, at Gran's party," Celine says, glancing at me.

"Yeah," I agree, leaning back in my chair, having polished off two tacos. "Bea did an incredible job with the party."

"You doubted her?"

"Nah." I shake my head and unwrap my third taco. "It's just weird sometimes; she's all grown up now. Got a boyfriend—"

"Cole's a good guy."

"Cole's one of the best guys I know. And I'm happy he and Bea are serious about each other." My gaze flicks to Celine's. "You know she's opening her store before Thanksgiving?"

Celine grins. "Yeah. I'm happy I'll be here for the grand opening."

"Me too," I agree quietly, meaning it. "I didn't realize y'all were in touch all these years, but thank you for looking out for her."

A flicker of pain zaps through Celine's eyes and she blinks

it away. "You don't have to thank me, Beau. I've always adored Bea, right from the beginning." She laughs. "What was she? Must have been—"

"Seven," I supply. "The first time you came to the house, Bea was seven. She wanted you to play—"

"Barbie!" Celine gushes, laughing. "God, I forgot about that. You were so annoyed."

I wipe salsa from my mouth and shake my head. "I was trying to lay down my moves and—"

"Your moves?" Celine hoots. "What moves? We were twelve!"

"I still had moves; I was on the hockey team."

Celine throws an arm out, all exaggeration and big personality. God, I missed this. Missed her. "Yeah, *hockey*. Not football."

I scowl and take a massive bite of my taco. She laughs.

"So," I say after a beat, "tell me about this movie. Oscar-worthy, huh?"

Celine blushes and dips her head. Hesitantly, she says, "It's a different character than I've ever played before. This film is a drama, with an edge of suspense. My character is Carley, a woman running away from an abusive relationship. A string of them really. She's tough and complicated, layered."

"Magdalena was layered," I object, referencing the character—a powerful sorceress—Celine played for nearly seven years.

Her eyebrows fly off her face. "You watched *Midnight Moon*?"

I huff. "Of course, I watched it. It was a national sensation."

Celine's lips curl into a wide smile.

"It's all anyone talked about," I continue. "Even in the barracks."

She tips her head back and laughs, exposing the graceful line of her neck. I tear my eyes away, focus on my taco.

"Besides, I wanted to see you in action."

"And?" Her laughter dies, her eyes serious on mine.

"And…" My voice cracks. I clear my throat. "You were incredible. Really."

An expression I can't describe travels over Celine's face. It makes her skin glow, as if a spotlight was flicked on, radiating from the inside out. Her beauty is so damn blinding. "That means a lot to me. That you watched. That you thought I was good."

"You've always been good. You know that."

She bites her bottom lip. "I remember you rehearsing lines with me."

"*Guys and Dolls*," I mutter, recalling the play our high school performed our senior year.

"*Guys and Dolls*," Celine confirms. She opens her mouth to say something when her phone rings.

It skitters on the table, between us, and my throat closes as I read the name on the screen.

Charlie.

Is Charlie a guy or a woman? Is it a professional or personal relationship?

My stomach tightens.

Why does it matter? It shouldn't.

Celine silences the call, and I don't know if that pleases or disappoints me.

Does she want to take the call and feels like she can't, because I'm here? Or it is unimportant?

She looks back at me and whatever she reads in my expression causes her to apologize. "Sorry."

I shake my head. "If you need to take that—"

I'm cut off as the phone buzzes again.

Celine sighs and picks it up. "Hey. Now's not a great time; I'm busy. I'll call you before bed, okay?"

Bed. The word glares in my mind like an obnoxious, blinking sign.

So, it's a man. It's personal.

A strange numbness sweeps my limbs, making my body feel heavy even though my mind lurches, wanting to get the hell out of here. Fight or flight.

But Celine dating isn't a dangerous situation; it's reality. It's something I've known for years.

I draw in a breath, knowing I'm overreacting. Logically, I'm fully aware of it. But my body reacts in a different way; my mind wants to shut down. I ball a paper napkin in my hand, focus on the way it crinkles.

"Yeah. Talk later." Celine ends the call. She places down her phone and looks at me. "Sorry."

"Don't be," I reassure her. My voice sounds too high. Too tight. I drop the napkin and flatten my hands against my thighs, wiping them on my jeans. "I should get going anyway." I stand awkwardly, tearing my eyes away from Celine's half-eaten taco.

I should sit down and wait for her to finish eating. God, Gran would twist my ear for this. But my adrenaline is in overdrive, even though my feet tingle with pins and needles.

I really need to go. Bounce.

"Um, okay?" Celine says awkwardly, shifting to her feet.

"This was—"

"Normal," she supplies.

I chuckle, the sound edgy. "Yeah." I dip my head. "Normal. We can be normal."

She smiles and it's sunshine, a big, bright beam of warmth. "I would like that."

Does she mean friendly? Or just…normal?

Again, does it matter?

I dig my keys from my pocket. "I'll see you around, Celine."

"Yeah," she agrees, following me to her front door.

"Thanks for the tacos. And the alarm system. And for fixing the lock on my door."

"Make sure you set it after I go," I say seriously.

She nods, her dark eyes holding mine. "I will."

"'Kay." I grip the back of my neck. I wish I was strong enough to stay. I wish I could do this with her, have her in my life in some capacity that isn't this temporary, fleeting thing. I shake my head at the thoughts. "Good-bye, Celine."

"'Bye, Beau." Her voice is soft.

I scurry down the steps and retreat to my truck, pushing the gear stick into drive and backing away from Celine's place. From the memories and the hurt and the girl who still, even though I don't want to admit it, has a hold on me.

I drive away from the small town I was brought up in. Escape to my condo in a nondescript building in downtown Knoxville. Here, no one knows me. No one recalls my complicated history with the famous beauty. Here, I can disappear into my surroundings and exist.

Safely. Alone. The way I have for the past year.

The way I need to if I'm going to survive the next four months with Celine back in town.

SIX
CELINE

"WHAT'S GOING on between you and my brother?" Nosy Bea Turner asks, her tone casual, and therefore at direct odds with her words.

I halt, staring at her. But she doesn't stop her perusal of nail polish colors for our pedicures. In fact, she turns to me and holds up a deep purple. "What do you think for autumn?"

"I like it," I reply automatically.

Bea snorts. One eyebrow lifts. "You and Beau?"

"We're..." I trail off. What the hell are we? For so long, we were the hottest item around. Then, we were nothing. Now... "We're normal."

Bea laughs. It's not subtle or cute or demure. It's a big, ol' knee-slapping, her cheeks are turning red, guffaw. She bends over, bracing her hands on her knees, as she laughs hard enough to draw attention. I wave off the curious glances of other patrons.

Still, Bea's laughter is infectious. I chuckle as I grab her arm, pulling her upright. "Stop making a scene."

"Stop being hilarious," she shoots back.

I shake my head. "I'm not."

"Normal?" Her eyes are shining, half with amusement and half with the tears from her laughter. "You and Beau are many, many things but normal will never be one of them, my friend." She pats me on the back like I'm dense and need her reassurance.

I pop my shoulder to shake off her touch and she laughs again.

"Pick a color," she reminds me. I grab a nondescript blush and Bea wrinkles her nose. "Boring."

I shrug. "I'm on set this week; they're going to change the color anyway."

"Then why are we getting pedicures?"

"Because I want to spend time with you."

"We could have gotten coffee."

"But mani and pedis used to be our thing," I remind her, desperate to recreate these old moments I used to take for granted.

Bea looks at me for a long moment before shrugging. "Okay."

I grin, then swap my boring neutral for a vibrant neon green.

Bea laughs and wraps an arm around my waist. "I missed you, Cece."

"Me too." I kiss the top of her head. "Come on, it's our turn."

Bea and I settle into pedicure chairs at the end of the row. A few women glance in our direction but for the most part, no one pays us attention. And I'm grateful. This is how it used to be, before most of America knew my name. Just me and Bea hanging out and talking about her brothers.

I lean back in my chair and dip my feet into the hot bath, letting out a sigh and closing my eyes. "Heaven."

Bea snickers. "I'm with you. It's been bananas trying to get everything ready for our store opening. I've been on my feet twenty hours a day."

"How's that going?" I turn to look at her.

Her eyes light up, pale grey. "It's going. I'm so excited, Celine. It's like everything I've been working toward, hoping for, is finally happening." She leans closer and drops her voice. "It's nerve-wracking."

"Yeah," I agree, knowing exactly how she feels. "Like too good to be true?"

"Exactly. I keep waiting for it all to unravel."

"Don't. Enjoy it; enjoy this time. You earned this, Bea. There's always going to be ups and downs, but don't let the fear of succeeding hold you back from doing it. Or enjoying it when it falls into place."

"Yeah…" she sighs, leaning back in her chair. "Easier said than done."

That's the truth. An old memory, one filled with my shrieks and racing heartbeat, high on adrenaline and possibility, rolls through me. It was a year after I moved to LA. Beau and I were still trying to figure out our future. We'd technically broken up but were still talking about a future together, exchanging letters and cards while he was at basic training, random text messages and emails. He surprised me, showed up at my apartment with flowers and a heartbreaker grin.

We spent the day together, laughing and reminiscing and *being*. At dinner, we ordered takeout and sat in my living room. We started talking about the future. About the life we were going to build. In our heads, it was simple. He could be a soldier and I could be an actress and we could have the happily-ever-after. Our year apart only proved how much we should be together. It made sense; we made sense.

Then, my phone rang. It was my agent with the role of a lifetime, Magdalena in *Midnight Moon*. I jumped up from the table, raced into my room, and started pulling out suitcases.

Beau stood in my doorway, his expression tight. Sure, he was happy for me but also, I think it was the moment he realized we didn't make as much sense as we thought.

Midnight Moon changed my life overnight. I went from a no-name nobody to America's sweetheart. But I don't recall a moment since then when I was living in a moment, just *being*.

Bea's phone rings and she takes the call. "Hey, Beau."

My eyes fly to hers. She wags her eyebrows at me. Busted.

"Normal, my ass," she mouths to me.

I stick out my tongue.

"Yeah, that's fine. I'm getting a pedicure with Celine right now."

I raise my eyebrows back, silently asking why she's bringing me up in the conversation. She blows me a kiss in reply.

"Let me check." Bea covers the mouthpiece of her phone. "Are you busy Wednesday night?"

"Why?"

"Gran's hosting a dance class at her place. All my brothers will be in town, and it would be fun for you to come."

I laugh. How can I not? God, I love Gran. I love that her grandkids all entertain these ideas too. I pull out my phone and check my schedule. "Wednesday, I have read-throughs during the day, but that's it. I'm free after six."

"Perfect." Bea removes her hand. "She's in. Yep, okay. See you later, Beau." She hangs up and grins at me. "Gran's going to be psyched that you're coming."

"Me too," I agree.

Bea and I catch up on the news about our families. She tells me about Brody and Blake's new business venture and explains that they're in Tennessee more frequently to meet with investors. I remind her that I see them from time to time when they're visiting LA. Even though Beau and I haven't spoken much in years, his family never cut me out the way he did.

Now, we're striving for normal, and it feels right.

I SMOOTH one hand down my flowy dress, the other holding a pie, as I stand on Gran's porch. I have no idea what kind of a dance class this is but I'm ready. Salsa, tango, ballroom, I'm Gran's girl. And the Turner family knows Celine Hernandez always brings it.

That's why when Bodhi pulls open the door, he whistles. "Looking good, Hernandez."

"Thanks, Bodhi." I hug him hello, careful not to crush the pie box. "What are you doing here? I thought your fans are loath to let you leave Miami."

He chuckles. "My fanbase is considerably smaller than yours so I can sneak away every now and then. And I'm here for work anyway. Doing a piece for one of the Coyotes." He mentions the NFL football team that is the soul of Tennessee sports. "We're doing some drawing concepts tomorrow and since the season started, it was easier for me to come here."

"And catch a dance class with Gran?"

"Girl, you know how it goes." He winks, his smile growing as he takes the pie from my hands. "You love me best, don't you, Cece?" He teases me the way he used to when we were younger.

I snort. "You know my answer is always Bea. Followed by Gran."

Bodhi laughs.

Gran runs the show and her doting grandsons and lovely granddaughter fall in line. It's something I've always admired about their family. Even with the loss and grief and pain they all experienced, they found a way to band together. Their sorrow made them stronger. The Turners are a true team in a way most families aren't. Irrevocably and unconditionally.

I step into the warm house and am immediately greeted by the Turner twins.

"Y'all are here too?" I hug Brody and Blake. "Bea said you'd all be in town but part of me didn't believe it until now."

"We've been spending more time on this side of the country," Brody explains.

"The lenders we're talking to are based in DC," Blake jumps in.

"Charging an arm and a leg in interest," Brody mutters.

My eyes dart between them as I try to keep up. "Bea filled me in a bit on your health care tracking app. Something about a bitcoin—"

"Blockchain," Brody corrects gently.

"And a smart thing—" I continue.

"Contract," Blake supplies.

"Right." I place my hands on their shoulders and squeeze. "Y'all lost me but I'm super proud of you."

"It's cause we're your favorites," Blake says knowingly.

"Please," Bea interjects, shoving her brothers out of the way to pull me into a hug. After a tight squeeze, she looks down at my toes and beams. "They didn't make you take it off!"

I laugh and flash her my hands, wiggling my fingers. They're now a perfect French manicure. "Nah, just my nails."

"Lucky!" Bea seems relieved that my pedicure didn't go to waste, and her thoughtfulness makes me want to pull her into another hug.

"Celine's here!" Gran announces.

"Now the party can start, right, Gran?" I hug her tightly and kiss her cheek.

"Exactly. Wait till you meet my dance partner," she whispers. "The old biddy in the corner, Mildred, thinks she stands a chance."

My eyes dart over Gran's shoulder to a lovely, elderly woman with hearing aids and a cane.

"You see how close she's speaking to him?" Gran mutters.

I glance at the elderly gentleman, looking debonaire in a linen blazer. "I like his pocket square. Very dapper."

"And her?" Gran presses.

I pull back slightly. "Gran, I think she's speaking close to him because of her hearing aids."

"Must've not turned 'em up," Gran sighs, exasperated. Her eyes roll so hard I'm surprised they don't get stuck.

I cough to cover up my laughter.

"It's okay. We all know she's trying to score with the Silver Fox," Brody says.

Gran gives him dagger eyes. Her hand darts out and twists his ear. "Language, Brody Jacob."

"Ow!" Brody swats her hand away.

This time, my laughter can't be contained. "I miss y'all," I admit to Brody.

He wraps an arm around my shoulder, and it feels comfortable. Familiar. "We miss you too."

The back door slides open and Beau walks in. He holds out a hand to the Silver Fox, who must be pushing ninety, and respectfully tips his head closer to the man.

Maybe he speaks softly? Poor Mildred might have incurred Gran's suspicion just by being polite.

Beau moves around to retrieve a cold bottle of water. He pours it into a glass and hands it to Mildred, chuckling at something she says.

My chest squeezes.

He looks good. A plain navy T-shirt that tugs across his chest and back when he moves. An old, worn-in pair of jeans. White sneakers and a white Thunderbolts baseball cap.

But it's more than that. He moves with confidence; he listens thoughtfully; he speaks truthfully. Beau Turner is more than a good man; he's the best man I know.

My heart remembers him as clearly as my memories. Being here, surrounded by his family, with Brody's arm on my shoulder and Bea's laughter in my ear, I miss this. Me with this family.

Beau looks up and his eyes latch onto mine. They darken, a lick of heat flaring. He straightens to his full height. He points me out to Mildred who gives me a sweet smile and a little wave.

I wave back but I can't tear my eyes from Beau.

Gran claps her hands and introduces the dance instructor. The music starts and couples take the makeshift dance floor.

Beau moves toward me. My heartbeat rings in my eardrums.

Cole swoops Bea into his arms. Brody is pulled away.

Beau stops in front of me, the tips of his sneakers nearly grazing my neon green toes.

"Hey," I say.

"Hi," he murmurs. One of his large hands settles on my waist.

I tip my head back to see his expression but it's unreadable. His fingers dig tighter into my side, his other hand clasping mine. Our fingers lace together. And it's comfortable. Familiar. Right.

"Dance with me, Cece." He drops my old nickname, the one I haven't heard from his lips in years.

"Yes." My response is automatic. My body already moving in sync with his, desperate for this moment. For real.

For more.

Beau guides me into the center of the makeshift dance floor. Gran's furniture has been carried out or pushed to the perimeter. A dance teacher leads the lesson, calling out instructions.

But I don't hear any of her words.

Just the sound of my heartbeat, Beau's steady inhales, and this moment.

Us.

SEVEN
BEAU

SHE'S INTOXICATING. Confusing. Overwhelming.

Having Celine in my arms hits me with pangs of nostalgia, the kind that cuts deep. Phantom pains: a longing that is more intense than remembering. I've missed her; I've missed this. And yet, as her perfume invades my senses and the heat of her skin presses against my palms, images I don't want to recall bombard my mind.

The cries of women. The screams of children. The burning scent of flesh.

I squeeze my eyes against the mental assault. Against the twisted memories and tangled emotions they evoke.

Instead, I pull Celine closer. Grip her harder. A gasp falls from her lips, and I loosen my hold, feeling like an asshole. She doesn't need my shit; no one does. I start to step away when her fingers clench mine. She rests her cheek against my chest, her hair brushing over my shoulder, tickling the base of my throat.

She must hear the erratic beating of my heart—how can she not? It pulses in my eardrums like the staccato of gunfire. But she doesn't call me out. She doesn't pull away. She doesn't give me wide eyes and a pitying look. Instead, she leans into me, gives me the moment, the privacy to pull my shit together.

In the crowded room, in the center of Gran's makeshift dance floor, I do. For the first time in a long time, I don't retreat. I don't panic and make excuses. I feel the pain that rolls through me, and I reach for the moment. The present. My reality.

I fucking cling to it. Right now, it's a curvy beauty with thoughtful eyes and a heart that used to own mine.

Slowly, the images fade. The noise subsides. And it's me and Celine, our breathing, our heartbeats. It's us again and I feel it. The pull of home, the *knowing* of belonging.

It crashes down on me like a thunderbolt: instant and sudden and bright.

I heave out a sigh and Celine glances up.

"You okay, Beau?" Her voice is soft. Soothing. Melted caramel and honey.

I clear my throat. "Never better, Cece."

She smiles when I say her nickname. She smiles like everything is right in the world. Like my head isn't fucked up half the time. Like she doesn't live across the country.

She smiles like she used to, when we were still us.

It alleviates some of the longing in my chest. Like a pressure valve, that smile lets out some of the tension and I can breathe better. Easier.

I grin back at her, and Gran's stuffy living room falls away. The laughter and the chatter, Gran's side-eye at Mildred, Bodhi's teasing Bea, it all disappears.

It's just me and my girl. Old memories and intense feelings.

I drown in Celine's eyes, inky black and bottomless. Her smile slips, slowly, as intensity sparks in her gaze.

I'm drawn to her, pulled by a past too strong to forget and

a future too desperate to overlook. My hand cups her cheek and she turns into my palm, seeking and wanting the same way I search for her.

I bend slightly, my face arcing toward hers, my mouth descending on her luscious lips. Her breath whispers over my chin and I tilt my face downward—

"Kiss her already!" Brody interrupts the moment.

The twins begin to harmonize behind him, belting out the lyrics to *The Little Mermaid's* "Kiss the Girl" like they watched it this morning.

In all fairness, Bea did go through a phase. Ariel's bright red hair solidified the mermaid as Bea's favorite Disney princess and we all watched the film countless times, memorizing all the lyrics to all the songs.

But right now? In this moment? "You've gotta be fucking kidding me," I mutter.

Celine laughs. It's one of those real, deep belly laughs, that you can't fake and hearing it again makes me grin, my brother's antics momentarily forgotten.

Bodhi cracks up and continues to sing, pointing at me.

The twins laugh, draping their arms over Celine's shoulders and swaying with her as they pick up the chorus.

"Sucker." Cole slugs me in the arm, like he wasn't fucking pining for my sister, stalking Gran's front porch and penning Bea love letters just a few months ago.

I slug him back.

Gran scurries by, upending any chance of salvaging my moment with Celine.

"Celine, I need you," Gran whisper-hisses.

Celine's eyes widen as she waits for Gran's request.

Gran clutches onto Celine's forearm with the strength of an eagle. "You need to send Gary's granddaughter a message and—"

"Who's Gary?" Celine asks.

"My dance partner." Gran points.

"The Silver Fox. Keep up," Bodhi chastises.

Gran rolls her eyes.

Celine chuckles. "Send his granddaughter a message? Like a text."

Gran shakes her head and waves a hand. "The kind where you talk."

"A voice note?" Brody guesses.

"Or a video?" Blake asks.

"Oh, you kids and your technology. One of them," Gran decides.

"Okay," Celine agrees. "Is it her birthday?"

"I think so," Gran says, dismissively. "But make it a good one because I think this will get me in Gary's favor."

"You want to push Mildred out," Bodhi states, nodding his head like he knew the plan all along.

"Oh, for Pete's sake," Gran murmurs, her fingernails digging into Celine's arm. "Hurry, Celine. Mildred's on the move."

We all turn to watch as Mildred conveniently corners Gary, boxing him against the wall with her cane.

"Well played," Blake murmurs.

"She planned this," Gran sneers, moving much faster than her ninety years should allow. She tugs Celine with her. Celine turns at the last second, shooting me a look filled with such amusement that I laugh, and give her a wave.

"Aw." Brody slings an arm around my shoulder. "Old love."

"I don't think Gran's in love with Gary," I retort.

"He meant you," Blake clarifies from my other side.

I frown. "Isn't the saying 'young love'?" I shake my head. "I'm not in love."

Bodhi laughs. "It's young love when you're…young."

I flip him the bird.

"And it's old love when you've been in love before," Blake decides.

"You and Cece." Brody shakes his head. "I don't think y'all have ever *not* been in love."

"It's not like that," I say even as my heart rate intensifies.

Because I fucking like the shit my brothers are spewing. I like the way it sounds, me and Celine in love. *Again.*

Even if it's not real, even if it's not going to happen, a part of me, much bigger than I admitted, *wants* it to be true.

"Sure, it is." Bodhi shrugs.

"Always been like that," Blake reminds me.

We all watch as Gran pushes Celine into Gary's side, cutting Mildred off by pointing to Celine and gesturing for Gary's cell phone.

Celine looks half horrified and half intrigued, playing Gran's game exactly as she wants. Within a few minutes, Gary and Celine are chatting like old friends and Gran's redirected Mildred's efforts to another old-timer, Matteo.

When Gran flashes us a thumbs-up, we all avert our gazes and pretend that the sweet little old woman who raised us didn't just play an eighty-five-year-old woman to get closer to the Silver Fox.

"You gonna do something about it?" Blake calls me out.

"Nah," I mutter, not wanting to have this conversation.

In the moments after my brothers' interruption, I was annoyed. I could feel my anger building—why would they ruin my moment? Why did they have to interject?

But now, I see it for the blessing it is.

Was I really going to kiss Celine here? In the middle of Gran's living room during a dance lesson with the senior citizen crowd?

I would have ignited the gossip chain, of which my gran holds a leadership position.

Besides, "She's got someone."

At my clarification, all three of my brothers' heads swivel in my direction.

"Who?" Bodhi demands.

"How serious?" Blake asks.

"Since when?" Brody wants to know.

Bodhi shakes his head. "I don't buy it. The way she was looking at you, man…"

"Y'all got unfinished business," Blake murmurs.

I shrug, leaving it alone. "It is what it is."

"It's something all right," Brody agrees.

I sigh, wanting to steer the conversation in a new direction. Luckily, Bea walks by and when she sees us in a huddle, she slows. "What are y'all up to?"

The twins grin and at Bodhi's nod, they all break into song again, whisking Bea away to dance.

I make my way over to the refreshments table Gran conned Cole into setting up and grab a Coke.

"You should've kissed her," Cole advises, slapping me on the back.

I chuckle as he walks away but once he's gone, my eyes find Celine. I watch her mingle with Gran, charm Gary, and leave a lot of voice notes for a lot of grandchildren.

She moves with grace, never in a hurry to extricate herself from a conversation. She seems genuinely pleased to fulfill the requests of Gran's dance class friends. Gran beams, proud as a peacock, probably disinheriting me and my siblings and claiming Celine as her favorite grandchild, as I sip on a Coke and stare at the woman who mesmerizes me.

I *should've* fucking kissed her.

"GOOD NIGHT, Y'ALL," Gran calls from the front porch as the last of her guests leave.

When she steps back inside, I close the front door after her and hold up my hand for a high five. She smacks my palm with hers. "You did it, Gran."

"It was fun, wasn't it?"

"More than I thought it'd be," I admit.

"Oh"—she flicks her wrist—"that's because Celine showed up. Otherwise, you would've moped."

"I did the foxtrot with you, didn't I?" I remind her.

She beams and pinches my cheek. "You certainly did, Beau. And you dazzled."

I laugh.

Gran smiles. "Miss that sound," she clucks, making her way into the kitchen. "Missed having this house bursting at the seams," she murmurs as she takes in the scene before us.

Bea is packing away leftover desserts. Celine and the twins are playing a game of cards, laughing and swearing at each other like they used to. Cole and Bodhi are moving the living room furniture back into place.

It's noisy and comfortable. Longing for what was rolls through me, stronger than before.

Celine's voice pulls my attention.

"You're a fucking cheater," she accuses Blake, jabbing a finger into his shoulder.

"Potty mouth," he retorts.

She flips him off and Brody snorts.

"Oh, how I've missed her," Gran remarks.

I lift an eyebrow. "What happened to calling everyone out for their 'language'?"

"Oh"—another dismissive wrist flick—"that's because I raised y'all. Don't want the neighbors to think you're heathens."

"Right."

"But Celine, she knows how to behave in public."

I snort.

Gran cuts me with a look. "She was good for you, Beau. And you were good for her."

"I know," I admit quietly.

Celine and I weren't just good together; we were fucking great. Relationship goals. Until life got in the way.

"What happened?" Gran whispers.

My family doesn't know the full truth of what went down between Celine and me. No one does; not even Celine.

Sure, they know that she moved to California, and I enlisted. They know we broke each other's hearts.

But they don't know that I went to LA a year later with my mom's engagement ring in my pocket. They don't know that I declared my love for Celine. That just when I planned to drop to one knee and propose, her phone rang. That she took the call, gutting me from the inside out, and that it was her agent with the biggest opportunity of her career. Celine screamed and started to pack, forgetting all about me.

Like I was already a distant memory. And then, I became one.

"Life," I say, not wanting to share all that with Gran. My humiliation and hurt are my own and I plan to keep them that way.

"Life," Gran says, her voice threaded with the wisdom and regrets of ninety years. She nods slowly and looks at me with sad eyes. "Sometimes life gives second chances."

"Sometimes," I say. *But this isn't one of those times.*

Gran stares at me knowingly. "You should've kissed her."

I shake my head, fighting the smile that wants to break free. "In your living room? Your friends would think you raised a heathen."

Gran laughs. "Oh, Beau. Did you see the way I was talking with Gary?"

I raise an eyebrow.

Gran shakes her head. "No one was looking at you."

At that, I toss my head back and laugh. It's one of those

big, deep, loud belly laughs and it pulls the room up short. Conversations halt and everyone stares at me.

Gran grins. "Missed that sound."

"Me too," I murmur, but I'm lost in two inky, bottomless pools of hope.

I should've kissed her.

EIGHT
CELINE

"I'LL FOLLOW YOU HOME," Beau says as the screen porch door bangs shut.

"Is that what you're calling it these days?" Gran cracks up, her bright eyes appearing on the other side of the screen.

Beau stuffs his hands into his pockets and leans back on his feet. He ducks his head, his neck turning red with embarrassment.

"Stop breaking his balls, Gran," Brody advises.

Gran's neck turns faster than a paparazzo with a zoom lens. "Language, Brody Jacob."

"And she says she's hard of hearing," Bea jokes.

Beau snorts. "Can someone close the door?"

Bodhi appears through the screen. He crosses his arms, leans casually against the doorframe, like he has all the time in the world. "Are you trying to have a moment alone?"

Beau sighs in exasperation but I laugh. I forgot how much fun the Turners are. I forgot the easy way they draw me into their cluster, claiming me as one of their own. Years ago, I thought I needed more; I wanted something *different*. Now, it's clear I was a fool. I *had* it all; I just didn't appreciate it then.

"You love me best." Bodhi grins victoriously at my laughter. "I always knew it."

"Close the door," Beau commands.

Bodhi faux sulks and shoots me a wink before giving in to Beau's demands.

Before any more of his family members can pop up, Beau takes my hand and guides me down Gran's front steps. He walks me to the waiting black BMW. My driver, Alfred, and my security guard, Caleb, chat beside it.

Unfortunately, my security team didn't think my driving myself around was the best idea. Without their endorsement, I passed on buying a new car and am driven everywhere like a child. My barely used driver's license remains tucked into my wallet.

I slip inside the back seat. Alfred and Caleb sit in the front and Alfred turns on the car.

With one hand holding the top of my door, Beau leans inside. "I'll follow you home."

"I'm sure I'll be fine," I give him the out, gesturing to the two men sitting up front. I don't want him to feel obligated to look out for me, to do all the little, thoughtful things he did when we were dating. Like follow my car home after a late night out. Or bring me morning coffee when I had a big exam.

Beau always went above and beyond—another thing I learned too damn late.

A pained expression flashes across Beau's face, quickly followed by exasperation. He pinches the bridge of his nose. "Be right behind you, Cece."

"Okay," I agree, my breath shaky.

His scent—fresh and clean, like laundry detergent and pinecones—wafts off him and wraps around me. I breathe it in, memorize it. Tonight hit me in my feels—too much remembering, too much nostalgia. Why don't we ever appreciate what is until it becomes what was?

Beau gives me a sharp nod and closes the back door.

Alfred eases out of Gran's driveway, with Beau's truck close behind. Beau trails us to my rental, parking in front and following me up the walkway. We say good night to Alfred and Caleb.

Once we're inside, I deactivate the alarm and Beau has a quick look around, as if a paparazzo is going to jump from a closet door. I remember him as protective but now, his actions are edged in paranoia.

Did a singular event in Afghanistan change him? Or was it an accumulation of all his years in service? Did his sacrifices chip away at his easygoing personality? Or did a moment, suspended in time, push him to the edge? When does anxiety become panic?

"You're all set," he declares, as if I was worried about it. As if Caleb doesn't regularly sweep the property and premises.

"Thanks," I say. I tip my head toward the kitchen. "Want a tea?"

A small smile hugs the corners of his mouth. "Peach?"

I nod, liking that he remembers that about me.

"Sure," he agrees, shuffling over to the kitchen island.

I fill the kettle and set out two mugs. "Tonight was fun."

He scoffs. "Gran's out of control."

I laugh. "Did you see her with Mildred?"

"Did you see her try to one-up Mildred by introducing you to Gary?"

I crack up, nodding. The kettle whistles and I pour two mugs of tea, placing one in front of Beau.

"Thanks," he mutters.

"Gary's sweet. He's completely oblivious to Gran's meddling."

"Manipulating," Beau corrects. "Poor guy."

I grin and shake my head, taking a small sip of my tea. "It was really nice to see the boys."

Amusement flares in Beau's eyes. "They're all in their twenties now. Bodhi's entire body is nearly inked."

"I know," I admit. "But I still see them as little kids, playing baseball and painting their faces for Halloween."

Beau's eyes hold mine, solemn. "You made that time, after"—his voice cracks and I know he means the immediate years after his parents passed—"more bearable. For all of us."

I lean over the kitchen island and place my hand on his. "Your family was like family to me."

"Yeah," he agrees.

"You still are," I admit.

His eyes sharpen on mine. Waiting.

I squeeze his wrist once before I straighten. "I realized it tonight." I wrinkle my nose, reaching for levity. "I miss the Turners."

Beau smirks. "Even Bodhi?"

"Yeah," I laugh. "Even Bodhi."

"You miss anything else?" he asks after a beat. His tone is light, but his eyes are serious, searching my face intently.

"Yeah." My voice is soft. "I miss this, Beau." I gesture between us. "Me and you."

"Us," he murmurs.

"Us."

Beau shifts in his chair. He places down his mug and stands, rounding the kitchen island until he's standing in front of me. I don't shuffle back, just turn into him. My lower back rolls along the edge of the island and one of Beau's hands grips the lip, keeping me between the island and his frame. My heart beats frantically, my skin tingles, desperate for his touch. I haven't craved a man like this since I was last with Beau Turner. It's always been *him*.

His grip on the island slips and his hand finds my waist instead. His palm lingers there, the heat of his skin pressing into my side. His other hand lifts, his fingers tilting my chin up. I lick my bottom lip and Beau's mouth parts, his eyes widening.

My stomach knots; my adrenaline spikes. I let out a shaky exhale. I want to demand Beau explain every thought running through his mind as much as I want to close my eyes and feel every second of this moment with him, no explanation necessary.

Beau's hand slides up my face and cups my cheek. His movements are steady, his eyes searching.

What do you want from me?

The words are loud in my mind, but I don't voice them. I don't say anything.

"I miss us too," Beau admits after a long moment.

Then, his mouth dips over mine. I lift my chin higher. My eyes flutter closed. His grip on my waist tightens.

Beau kisses me slowly. It's half of a memory and half of the unknown. It's entirely intoxicating. After our lips brush against each other's twice, he deepens our connection. He steps more firmly against me, our bodies pressing together. And God, does he feel good.

My one hand grips the edge of the island, giving me leverage to push against Beau's hard planes. My breasts flatten against his chest and his arm wraps firmly around my waist, tugging me closer.

Beau's tongue slips into my mouth and meets mine in a dance we've done a thousand times, but the steps are different now. This isn't old, familiar, easy Beau. It's new and exciting. Thrilling.

As his hand flattens against my lower back, I arch into him, and nip at his bottom lip. A chuckle falls from his throat as he kisses me harder, taking our kiss from sweet to steamy in a heartbeat.

My arms wrap around his back, my hands exploring the planes of his body. He's ripped now, all cut muscle and pure strength. His hands clasp my waist and easily lift me onto the edge of the island. He tugs my knees apart and steps between them, picking up where he left off. But now, his body hovers over mine, giving me more connection, more friction, more him.

And I revel in it.

As Beau presses into me, my hands move behind me, planting on the kitchen island and holding me up, as my legs wrap around his waist.

I kiss him with a desperation that's been missing from every hookup I've had since he last kissed me good-bye. Beau's mouth leaves my mouth and drags down my neck, hot and needy. I tighten my legs around his waist, whimpering when his hard length brushes against my core.

I clench him harder, wanting to escalate things. Right now, I want Beau to take me on the kitchen island and make me remember everything I've never truly forgotten with perfect clarity. I grind myself against him, my moan more wanton this time and Beau…stops.

"Fuck," he mutters, hanging his head. His hands are rooted on either side of my hips.

Realizing I took it too far, pushed him too much, I try to scoot back. In doing so, I knock over his tea mug. "Shit," I swear as the hot tea burns my hand. The mug clatters to the floor, shatters.

Beau springs into action.

"Beau!" I holler as he swiftly lifts me, turns me, cradles me against his chest and keeps me there as he lowers us to the ground.

In one moment, I went from sitting on the island to sitting in Beau's lap on the floor.

He heaves out a deep sigh and taps the back of his head against the kitchen cabinet. I try to move but his hand holds my thigh, keeping me rooted to his lap. He shifts me in his arms, gentling his hold.

"Are you okay?" he asks seriously. The heat of a few

moments ago is gone, drenched in the cold reality that he's worried about the mug of tea. As if demonstrating my point, he gently lifts my hand. "I'm sorry, Cece."

I shake my head. "It's nothing. I'm fine. Besides"—I successfully wriggle out of his lap. He stands up beside me and flips on the faucet, guiding my hand under the cool water —"it was my fault." I glance at him over my shoulder, hating the pain and worry in his eyes.

"No," he disagrees. He moves to the refrigerator for an ice pack. "I took it too far. I shouldn't have—"

"I wanted you to," I cut him off.

He glances from the island to the floor where we were just sitting. He sighs again. "I'm fucked up, Celine. My head is… I'm all over the place."

I turn off the faucet and move closer to him. Lacing my fingers with his, I press our palms together. "That's not true. You were right there with me until I broke the mug."

He chuckles darkly. "Most days, I need a fucking anti-anxiety pill to get through the hours."

I shrug. "A lot of people need support in a lot of different ways, Beau. There's no shame in that."

Beau's eyes are unreadable, his expression grim. He watches me closely, studying me again.

What are you looking for?

Again, I don't voice my thought.

Beau shakes his head and presses the ice pack against my hand. "Let me clean this mess up."

"I've got it." I start to move toward the broken mug, but Beau throws out an arm.

"Please. Let me." At the pain in his tone, I stop. I clutch the ice pack against my hand.

He cleans the mess up quickly, asking for my vacuum at the end to make sure he picks up every shard of ceramic.

After placing the vacuum back in the closet, Beau turns to me. I drop my ice pack on the counter and show him my hand. Even though the skin smarts, it's just a surface burn. "All better."

He doesn't smile. Instead, he stuffs his hands in his pockets.

"I can make more tea," I offer.

His eyes flash to mine, more pained than relaxed. "I should get going."

My stomach knots for an entirely different reason at the forlorn expression on his face. Why won't he let me in? Why won't he *talk* to me?

"Okay," I say finally, walking toward the front door and pulling it open for him. "Thanks for tonight, Beau." My eyes dart back to the kitchen before finding his again. I smile. "I really had fun."

The darkness that clouded his features has lightened and he offers me a small smile. "Me too, Celine. For a minute there..." He shakes his head, grips the back of his neck. "It was like it was us again."

"Yeah," I agree. *Can we still be us?*

Not if we don't talk about the past. About what happened to us as a couple, about the ways we've changed as individuals. But at the pain in Beau's eyes, coupled with his confession, the last thing I want to do is make him more anxious. I don't want to rock the boat when we're finally coasting together again.

Beau steps out onto the porch. "Lock up—"

"I will," I say before he can finish.

He watches me for another beat, and I wish I understood what his looks mean. What he's thinking. What he wants.

"Good night, Celine."

"Night, Beau."

He bounds down the steps and jogs over to his truck, as if he needs to put space between us. As if he needs to create distance between himself and the moment we shared in the kitchen.

I lift my hand in farewell as he drives off.

Then I close my front door, lock up for the evening, and set the alarm.

I pour myself a second mug of tea and sit down at the island.

What did tonight mean? What does any of it mean?

Will Beau and I ever be an us again? Can we?

NINE
BEAU

I SHOULDN'T HAVE KISSED her.

It's the only thing that makes sense, the only thing that explains why I spent the night plagued by horrors. Even now, in the morning light, I still feel the heat of fire singeing along my arm, around my shoulder, and down my spine. I hear the echoes of Ramirez's howls. The lights are blinding and then, the darkness descends, plunging me into a despair so deep, light is laughable.

Fuck. I try to shake off the terror that grips me. I've thrown up twice already and am trying, again, to eat a bite of toast before practice. I breathe in, hold it, slowly exhale. Reach for my medication but hold off, desperate to regain control on my own.

I breathe in again, trying to calm my anxiety, to ease the cold sweat that beads along my hairline.

I shouldn't have fucking kissed her.

I crossed a line. I started to hope. To think I could be normal. That I could be capable of sharing something good, something sweet and real and true, with a woman who I feel too many damn things for.

I kissed Celine and the worst moments of my life came

back to haunt me. The mission that went sideways. The men that we lost. The women and the children and the fucking wreckage and despair.

Bile climbs up my throat and I make it to the kitchen sink just in time to spew out a stream of water. Nothing in my stomach and I still can't keep shit down. Buried. It's all coming up. The repressed memories, the horrible feelings, the fucking fear.

And Celine? She's all good. Pure-hearted, sincere, sweet like honey. All I'd do is taint her, drag her down into my messed-up shit with my fucked-up head.

I take a swig of water straight from the faucet, swish it around my mouth, spit. Relocating to the bathroom, I brush my teeth and take a shower, trying to rinse off the emotions that cling to my skin, sticky and constant. Always right there, just below the surface, impossible to shake.

I drag my ass to the arena for practice but I'm off. My head is all over the place, my body is so exhausted, it aches.

I shouldn't have kissed Celine and all I can think about is doing it again. Hearing the little noises she makes, so different than the ones she used to moan. Less hesitant now. Feeling the press of her heat up against me. Running my fingertips over the softness of her skin, the swells and dips of her curves.

I bang my fist against the shelf in my locker.

"What the fuck's wrong with you?" River Patton asks.

I turn my head, look at my teammate who always acts like he's carrying a chip so big, it may as well be a fucking crater, on his shoulder, and glare. "Worry about your own shit," I tell him.

The noise behind me, the general conversation and sounds of the guys suiting up for practice, comes to an abrupt stop. I hang my head. Fuck.

Rein it in. Get your shit under control. Bury it. Deeper.

I've never lost my cool with the team before. Nor with my

family. I don't do shit like that. I'm even-keeled. I'm level-headed. I'm *fine*.

Afghanistan may have fucked me up, but no one here needs to know it. Not when I'm living my dream. Hell, I'm a fucking NHL player. I get to do the thing I used to talk about, when we were on night patrols, when we were bored out of our minds. When we were scared as shit and making conversation just to pass the time, I get to do the thing, the passion, I shared with my team.

Ramirez didn't get to open a tattoo parlor.

Henley didn't buy a motorcycle.

Roberts never even met his baby girl.

I'm supposed to be grateful. I'm supposed to be *living*. I'm supposed to kiss my girl.

My hand curls into a tighter fist. I bang the locker shelf again.

I'm unraveling and I can't do it here. Not when I swore to the guys I'd make it. I'd do it big for all of us. I'd live the fucking dream.

The fucking dream that feels simultaneously incredible and awful.

The fucking dream that can't include Celine because what can I offer other than night terrors and paranoia?

"Turner." Axel Daire, the biggest guy on the team, steps up beside me.

I see him in my peripheral vision, but I don't turn. Because a swell of emotion is replacing the blaze of anger. It rushes behind my face, swells in my eyes, makes my nose itch.

I want to cry. No, not cry, wail. Grieve.

And I can't do that here either.

"Hey, man." Devon Hardt, our team captain, steps up on my other side.

From the sounds behind me, I know the rest of the team is filing out. Devon must've signaled for them to leave and for that, I'm grateful. If I'm going to fall apart, I'd rather minimize the number of teammates who witness it.

Roberts comes to mind. When he heard that his wife was pregnant. She recorded the whoosh-whoosh of the baby's heartbeat and sent it to him and man, he fucking lost it. Broke down and sobbed in the middle of Kandahar. The silent kind, that doesn't make noise but causes your shoulders to shake.

That's the fucking shit I feel like doing right now. It's gripping me, the sadness, the unbearable weight of it all. It's making the veins on my forearms stand out. It's causing a buzz to drum in my head.

My mouth is dry, so dry swallowing is difficult.

Get your shit under control. Bury it. Deeper.

"What's going on, man?" Daire tries.

"Talk to us," Devon commands.

I breathe in, hold it, let it out slowly.

I close my eyes, think of Celine. Her sweet noises. Her hot mouth. Her delectable body and the curves I want to memorize with my eyes, my hands, my tongue.

The pain recedes. The hurt dulls. I pull in another breath, manage a swallow. My hands relax and the buzz in my mind quiets.

Celine. Celine. Celine.

I fucking kissed her.

I smile. Glance at Daire. Shrug. Look at Hardt. Shake my head.

Bury it. Deeper.

"I'm fine. Really." I hold my hands up in apology. "Just got a lot of shit going on; I didn't sleep well."

Daire crosses his arms in front of his chest, his biceps bulging. He watches me carefully. I glance at Devon. His jaw ticks, silently calling me out on my bullshit. But he doesn't say anything.

I grab my helmet. "I won't bring my shit into the locker room again."

Deeper.

"Come on." I step around them. "We've got practice."

I leave the locker room, ignore the rest of the team, and glide onto the ice.

The cool air feels good against my heated skin. The glide of my skates centers me. The weight of my gloves allows me to stretch my fingers.

I let out a breath filled with relief.

I reined it in. I buried it. I kissed Celine.

I got this. I'm fine.

TRAFFIC IN DOWNTOWN Knoxville is worse than usual, but instead of swearing at the constant stops, I grin. It's because Celine's filming downtown today and while that may have irked me a few weeks ago, today, I'm hoping I get a glimpse of her the same as these other rubberneckers.

She's been working nonstop the past week. Still, she's managed to catch me off guard by having a breakfast delivered after one of my practices and showing up late one night with two peach teas and a box of doughnuts. She's making room for me in her life, in her crazy schedule, and it feels good.

I want to let her in. I want to spend time with her. God, even when I'm with her, I miss her.

All my excuses from last week don't hold the same weight. Now that the nightmares are back in full force, what's holding me back? What could possibly go wrong? If I'm already suffering, shouldn't I at least reach for the light Celine's presence provides?

Knowing she's here and not pulling her into the orbit of my life is a different kind of torture. It doesn't just heighten my nerves and play with my head, it makes me remember and yearn and crave. For the past that we shared and a future I'm unworthy of. For her breathless laughter and soulful eyes.

I squint as the sunlight glares through the windshield. For a second, I think I spot Celine but as I pass in front of some of the film trailers, I realize it's a staff member. Sighing, I drive the rest of the way home.

Once I shower and eat, I sit down on my couch, my phone in hand. Pulling up our thread, I send Celine a text.

BEAU

How did downtown treat you?

I don't expect an immediate response and I'm pleased when she answers a minute later.

CELINE

Amazing! It was like a homecoming.

BEAU

You're Tennessee's sweetheart.

CELINE

(Laughing emoji) Why are you flattering me?

BEAU

Can't a guy just be nice?

CELINE

A guy? Sure. But Beau Turner? You want something...

You.

The word lands in my mind like a grenade, only a matter of time before the truth explodes. But right now, the pin is in place, and I don't admit aloud how much I want to see her. How errant my thoughts have been since we kissed. How desperate I am to reconnect with her since we danced at Gran's.

I do.

After admitting she's right, I dial her.

"Hey!" she answers on the first ring, her voice cheerful.

"Good day on set?"

"Yes. We're filming one more scene and then wrapping for the day."

"Good. Is now a bad time?"

"Nope. I've got"—voices rumble in the background—"fifteen minutes."

"I'll make it quick then. I want to take you to dinner."

Celine's quiet for moment and I think I've surprised her. I keep my breathing even, try to slow my heart rate even as I clench my phone.

Will she say yes? Does she think our kiss was a mistake? Didn't she insinuate more when she showed up late at night?

"I'd love to." Her voice is husky, and it fills me with a swell of confidence. "And I'm sure Caleb will love a night off."

I grin. "Friday night?"

Muffled voices fill the line again and then—"I'm shooting until 8 PM. Can we aim for 9 PM or is that too late?"

"I can do nine," I say, relieved that my Saturday game is home with a 7:30 PM start. "I'll make reservations. Any preferences?"

"Nope. You know me." She laughs.

Do I still? I wonder but don't ask because the sound of her laughter makes my chest tighten. God, I still want to know her. I still want to be an us.

But can I work through the demons that haunt me? Can I fight the battles when Celine's presence, her damn sweetness, serves to remind me how unworthy of her laughter I am?

Fuck if I'm not gonna try. But how? How can I prove that we have a shot when half the time, I second-guess myself?

One day at a time. One hour. One step in front of the other.

In Afghanistan, the toughest days were broken down into manageable blocks of time. The worst moments, measured by heartbeats.

I blow out an exhale. A heartbeat.

"Okay," I say. "I'll pick you up from set on Friday."

"Sure. I'll message you once I'm done for the day."

"Good luck with your last scene, Hernandez."

"Bye, Beau."

I end the call and toss my phone down. Outside, dusk is settling. Golds and oranges reflect off the buildings. It looks so peaceful, a long, busy day coming to a conclusion.

Tiredness clings to the edges of my mind and my body feels heavy. Not with the usual soreness from hockey, but with the accumulated emotional weight of the past week. Of the past decade.

I shift on my couch and grab a throw pillow Daire's woman, Maisy Stratford, decorated my space with. She did the same shit to Damien Barnes and River Patton and while she's a good woman with a big heart, I think her soft touches to my bachelor pad are a waste. Not because I don't appreciate them but because my heart has only ever belonged to one woman.

Celine Hernandez.

On Friday, I'm getting another chance. A do-over.

One heartbeat, one step at a time.

The thought fills me with calmness and I close my eyes, drift off to sleep.

This time, the nightmares don't come and for that, I'm grateful too.

TEN
CELINE

"HE MUST BE SPECIAL," my costar, Thad Stevens, comments from the door to my trailer.

I meet his gaze from my perch on the bench. I need to put on my heels and spritz some perfume but otherwise, I'm ready for my date with Beau. I'm more than ready. "He is."

Thad grins, enters my trailer, and takes the seat across from mine. "This the high school sweetheart you never got over?"

I give him a look.

His grin widens. "The tabloids are talking."

"And you read them?"

He gives me a look of disbelief. As if there's something wrong with me for *not* reading untrue stories about myself. "Of course I read them. I love to know who the world thinks I'm shacking up with."

I laugh. "Who are you shacking up with this week?"

"A cowboy," Thad deadpans.

I shake my head. "I love how easygoing you are about... all of this." I gesture around the trailer.

"Fame?"

I nod.

He sighs. "It's all I've ever known. I grew up on movie sets."

"That's right. Both your parents were in the business."

"Yep. Mom was an actress and Dad was a director."

"And now?" I wonder.

"They're retired. Living their best lives in France."

"Your parents are the exception to the rule."

"Especially in this business," he agrees. In our world, scandals, divorce, cheating is all par for the course. But the Stevenses made it work.

"You turned out relatively normal," I add.

Thad tosses his head back and laughs. "I like you, Celine. You're not nearly as much of a diva as they make you out to be."

I roll my eyes. "I thought I was a sweetheart."

"You're not reading enough tabloids."

"Touché, Thad." I dip my head in his direction. "What are you doing tonight?" It's not common for us to have a Friday night to ourselves in the middle of filming.

He gives me look, a little gleam of amusement in his eyes. "A cowboy."

"Right." I smack myself in the forehead. It's only after a moment of charged silence that I realize Thad isn't joking. His sexuality has been a subject of discussion in several circles, but it isn't until this moment that I've given it any thought.

This moment, where Thad confides in me that he is indeed involved with a cowboy, at least for tonight.

"Oh," I say.

He grins. "Knew you were more than a pretty face, Hernandez."

I laugh. "I didn't know."

"I know. I prefer it that way. But, after working with you the past few weeks, I think you and I could actually be friends."

"In the real world?"

He nods.

"I'd like that," I say. I knew the moment I met Thad that filming a movie with him would be fun. He never makes me uncomfortable the way other male costars, some knowingly and others obliviously, have done in the past when filming intimate moments. He has a wicked sense of humor, although half the time I can't tell if he's serious or joking. And he's nice to everyone on set, going out of his way to remember people's names and wish them a good morning. "I'm going out with my high school sweetheart."

Surprise flares in Thad's eyes and I can tell he didn't expect me to be forthcoming about my plans. "So, it's true?"

"Most of it," I agree, not knowing the full extent of what the media has published about my high school relationship with Beau.

Thad's eyes scan me from head to toe. "You look beautiful."

"Thank you."

"Nervous?"

I let out a sigh. "More than I want to be."

"You still love him." He states it as fact, and I realize how transparent I am.

"I don't know if I ever stopped," I admit. It's strange to confide so much in someone I don't know that well, especially someone in the industry.

But Thad Stevens is known as a steel vault. In fact, he's so difficult to read that his sexual orientation isn't confirmed. The media hasn't been able to confirm any recent aspects of his life and that, coupled with his earlier admission, makes me confide in him.

"Those are the loves you hold on to," he says, his tone weighted with wisdom. "The ones that won't let you go. Don't fight that, Celine. Cling to it." The intensity in his eyes gives me pause, and I realize Thad must have his own heartbreak and regrets.

I clear my throat. "And the cowboy?"

He gives me a sad smile. "Just killing time."

I nod, reading between the lines. Thad has a past he hasn't moved on from and right now, any interaction is of the casual variety. Maybe like my arrangement with Charlie. It's something that feels good, consistent. It's something I can rely on without trusting all the way.

But it's not the real thing and because I've tasted real, anything else will always be imitation.

My phone buzzes and I glance at it.

BEAU

Here. No rush.

I smile at the message. It's so Beau. Direct, taciturn, efficient. I bend to put on my heels.

When I'm done, Thad extends a hand and I take it, allowing him to pull me up. He gives me a once-over and whistles. "Have fun tonight, Hernandez. Cling to that shit." He winks.

I grin and shake my head. "You too, Thad. I'll see you tomorrow."

Thad walks me out to Beau's waiting truck. When Beau spots us, he slips from the driver's side and rounds the front of the truck.

"Hey, man," Thad greets him, extending a hand. "I'm Thad."

"Stevens," Beau mutters. He shakes his head, as if embarrassed for his slipup. "I'm Beau Turner." He shakes Thad's hand.

Thad tilts his head, studying Beau. "Hockey?"

Beau grins. "Yeah. It's good to meet you."

"Same. Have a good night." Thad lifts a hand in farewell.

I slip into the passenger seat and buckle up. Beau waits until Thad re-enters his trailer before backing out of the lot. "I can't believe your costar is Thad Stevens."

"Yeah. He's a great guy," I comment. I usually have a positive working rapport with my colleagues. Charlie became a permanent fixture in my life after we worked together and a lot of the women I've collaborated with have become friends. But my connection with Thad holds an easygoingness that came instantly, without effort on either of our parts.

"One helluva actor," Beau adds. He glances over at me. "You look beautiful, Cece."

"Thank you."

"I'm sorry to inform you that you're going to be severely overdressed for where we're going."

My mouth drops open and a flicker of panic flames to life. "Where are we going?"

Beau gives me a lopsided smile. It's the same one he had in high school, and it warms my heart, seeing him now, at ease and playful when he's been so severe. "The Rib Shack."

I laugh, leaning back in my seat.

"Strickland's is closed for a private function," he explains, referencing the top steakhouse in Knoxville. "And I was thinking, where should we go? Wherever we go, people will recognize you. And I'm sure you're used to fancy restaurants and upscale wine bars. But when was the last time you had ribs?"

I bite my bottom lip, touched by his thoughtfulness because he's right. I am used to fancy restaurants and upscale wine bars. But, "I haven't had good ribs, hell, decent barbecue, in a long, long time."

"So, it's not just the tacos?"

I laugh. "No. My trainer's got me on a strict meal plan most of the time. I've been breaking the rules here."

Beau extends a hand and I take it, our fingers lacing together from muscle memory. "I want you to have fun, to enjoy your meal, more than I want to impress you," he admits.

"You always impress me," I tell him the truth.

A shadow passes through his eyes.

I shake my head. "Don't do that."

"Do what?" He turns back to watch the road.

"Get in your head. You've got things you're working through. I get that. So do I."

His eyes cut to mine again.

"Nothing bad," I reassure him. "Just...stuff. But I want to have fun again, Beau. I want us to be us."

A small smile flits across his lips. He doesn't say anything, just tightens his hold on my hand. We ride the rest of the way in comfortable silence. Downtown fades away as Beau drives us toward The Rib Shack, a staple in the town we were raised in.

He's wearing worn jeans and a Henley shirt. He looks relaxed and hot as hell. An old country song plays through the speakers, and I chuckle. Beau glances at me, gives a little smile.

I relax fully in my seat and stare out the window. How many times did I ride shotgun in Beau's truck? How many nights did we sit like this, his hand in mine, just driving around and singing off-key?

It's dark outside and I can barely make out the houses we pass since the roads are hardly lit. The farther we drive into the country, the darker it grows. My mind wanders back to high school and the forever I used to believe in when Beau was by my side.

I look at him, memorize the lines of his face, the shape of his chin, the angle of his cheekbone. He's a man now and still, I recall the heart of the boy with perfect clarity.

Beau Turner used to be a hopeless romantic. He was responsible and serious. But underneath his exterior was a loving, compassionate, caring kid who raised his siblings and gave everything in the name of service to those he loves. But more than that, he was mine.

Is he still that man? Could he ever belong to me again?

Would he even want me now? Would any man want a woman who travels for months at a time, who doesn't know what a home base feels like, who is constantly splashed across tabloids? Would a partner want a girlfriend, or wife, who lived with her feet in two different cities, sometimes two different countries?

Would Beau?

ELEVEN
BEAU

"YOU'VE GOT A LITTLE..." I scratch my chin.

Celine grins, her mouth filled with food, as she runs a napkin over her chin, catching the BBQ sauce.

I snort. "You're a mess, Hernandez."

She chews her mouthful and swallows. Takes a swig of Coke. "Some things don't change."

"What?" I shake my head. "You've got it together."

She leans forward, her eyes darting to the sides as if she's worried someone will overhear her. "It just looks that way. On the outside." Her tone is playful, but her eyes are serious, truthful. "On the inside, I'm all over the place."

I roll my lips together, regard her warily. Is she joking? Or are we taking a deep dive into a serious discussion? "All over the place, how?"

She cleans her fingers with a wet wipe and pushes her hair behind her ears. She wrinkles her nose the way she does when she's unsure of something. "Lost," she says finally. At the hurt in her voice, I realize we're scuba diving. I place down my rib and give her my full attention.

She's silent for so long that I prod. "Can you expand on that?"

She gives me a small smile. "All I've ever wanted was to be an actress."

"And you're an incredible actress."

"I love my career. I love the work I've done and I'm proud of it."

"You should be." I place my hand over hers, wondering where she's going with this.

"Then why does it feel like something's missing?" Her voice quivers as she voices the question.

I stare at her, noting the flecks of gold in her dark brown eyes. There's a sadness there I don't like. "Maybe something is," I say slowly.

"You know I spend most of my life surrounded by people."

I nod.

"And yet, coming back here made me realize how lonely I am. How most of my relationships, friendships, only exist at the surface level. Being at Gran's house...that dance party..."

"What?"

"I miss it. The woman I was when I lived here, and Tennessee. The Turner family." Her eyes shine with unshed tears, but she manages a smile.

"You're still that woman. I see you, all eager and enthusiastic. Still talking and smiling at everyone you pass. You're still *you*. And we haven't gone anywhere, Cece. Whenever you're in town, we're here. You can come to Gran's anytime. Hell, you can move in with her."

Celine laughs and dips her head in agreement. "I know. It's not that. It's the everyday things..." She shakes her head. Sighs heavily. Waves her hand. "Don't listen to me. I'm just feeling nostalgic. I have nothing to complain about and I realize how ridiculous I must sound—"

"Don't do that," I cut her off, frustration in my tone.

She frowns.

"Downplay your shit because you're living your dream. Your feelings still matter."

She dips her head in silent gratitude. She takes another sip of her Coke. "Look at us, being all normal and shit."

I chuckle. "We're adulting."

Celine snorts and I grin.

She picks up her ribs. We finish our meal in comfortable silence, but things feel different. More settled.

Whatever Celine and I are, it's confusing. And yet, I want to sort it out. With her, I want to fix all the shit going wrong in my head, all the things I've been ignoring.

"STILL OCEAN or have you moved onto mountains?" I ask as I drive back to her place.

I can feel her studying my profile, but I don't turn to meet her eyes. Tonight with Celine was my own kind of homecoming and I want to keep our connection going for as long as possible.

"Still ocean," she says softly. "I can't believe you remember that."

I grin, sliding my palm over the top of the steering wheel. "Really? All you talked about was—"

"Living on the beach one day—"

"And having a hammock—"

"To read in," she finishes, laughing. And then, "I don't have much time for reading."

I glance at her. "But you got a hammock?"

"Yeah," she says softly. "I wish I sat it in it more. The view from my place is spectacular. You would love it; well, maybe not *you*. Still worried about tidal waves and earthquakes?"

I snort, recalling my old fears. Back in high school, I didn't understand why anyone would want to live anywhere but Tennessee. Smoky Mountains and endless greenery. A kid could adventure on our land for an entire day and only experience a tiny speck of it. But my old fears have disappeared in the wake of new ones. "Nah, not anymore."

Celine continues to stare at me. "Gonna share any of these newfound fears?"

I snort and reach over to grab her knee, squeezing right above it where I know she's ticklish. On cue, she shrieks and tries to pry my hand away. "Beau!"

"It's not spiders or anything," I tell her, grinning. "Just, different things to worry about now, you know?"

My response was cryptic as hell but what am I going to say? I'm petrified of not living enough? Of letting down the guys I should have died with? Of hearing my sister, Bea, wail in the night with the same desperation of the women in those villages?

I shudder and try to shake off the clamminess that thoughts of Afghanistan bring. I'm relieved when I pull into Celine's driveway and cut the engine.

We sit in silence for a beat, both of us staring at the Klingers' place, seeing it through grown-up eyes, or maybe recalling the way it used to be. Filled with teenagers and a bonfire.

"You gonna walk me in?" Celine asks, cutting the silence. Her tone has that sexy husk to it again and I feel it move through my body like a current, lighting up parts of me that've been dormant for too long.

Of course, I haven't been a saint the past eight years. But I haven't hooked up with women to bury my thoughts and feelings either. I do that well enough on my own.

I unbuckle my seat belt and turn toward Celine. "I'll always walk you in."

She gives me a soft, knowing smile. I step out of the truck

and round the front, pulling open her door and helping her down. With her hand in mine, we walk up the path to her place.

The longing hits me square in the chest. What if this was real? What if this could be my life? I try to shake it away. I stopped believing in pipe dreams a long time ago—even though Bea would call bullshit since I've achieved my long-time dream of playing in the NHL. But my dreams with Celine are different.

One step in front of the other.

She unlocks the door, turns off the alarm, and lets me in so I can do a quick sweep. I feel better seeing her belongings as she left them. An empty mug on the kitchen island, her makeup brushes scattered on the vanity in the bathroom. The slippers by the side of her bed. Little indications that Celine lives here, that it's really her, settles something inside me that I don't fully understand.

She's pouring hot water into two mugs when I approach her in the kitchen.

"You like living here?" I ask, scratching the back of my neck.

Celine nudges one mug closer to me and I step up to the island, slide onto a barstool, and wrap my hand under the mug's handle.

Celine glances around the space. It doesn't contain any of her artwork or photographs and yet, it's her. The flowers in a funky vase Bea made. The handful of change in a little dish on the countertop. The tiny details, they're all her. "Yeah," she says, smiling. Her eyes find mine. "I really do."

I nod, unable to look away. Celine's eyes darken and it's as if she's trying to convey a thousand thoughts to me in a single glance.

I miss you. I still care about you. I want you.

But am I reading them correctly? I used to make decisions

without second-guessing, without holding back. Now, every decision I make requires careful consideration because...I don't trust myself to always make the right ones. The weight of one wrong move sits on my chest like a fucking anvil. Most days, I wish it would bury me completely.

"Beau." Celine's voice pulls me back to the moment.

She's rounded the island and is standing before me. I open my knees and she steps between them, lets me cage her in between my thighs. Her expression is thoughtful, eyes curious. All patience and understanding. Celine Hernandez is one of the best women I know.

Maybe that's why there's never been anyone else? How could there be?

Her hands find the tops of my shoulders and rest there. My hands travel up to her hips and hold.

"Penny," she whispers and one side of my mouth lifts in a smirk.

Penny for your thoughts, Beau Turner.

Her twelve-year-old voice, those chocolate eyes, the gleam of her metal braces, flashes through my mind.

I pull her closer and she comes willingly. Our eyes have an entire conversation, but our mouths don't move.

Kiss me. A plea.

If I do, I won't want to stop. My confession.

So don't. Her taunt.

Seriously? My quip.

Try me. A challenge.

The air around us is charged, almost electric. Like the air before a rainstorm in summer. Our gazes hold, our mouths parting.

And then, we move.

I lift my chin at the same time as Celine sinks into me. Her hands are around my neck, mine are around her waist, and our mouths collide.

This kiss isn't gentle or sweet.

It's a long overdue battle of wills. My fingers dig into the soft swells of her ass as she nips my bottom lip. I flatten my hand in the center of her back and her mouth parts, giving me access.

Our tongues invade each other's mouths, dueling.

Pent-up frustration. Old hurts, desperate words we never said. Our kiss is wrought with accusations we should've hurled and tears we never shared.

I fist Celine's hair, my knuckles pressing against the back of her head as I try to control the kiss. To show her how much I fucking want her. How much she hurt me. How much our breakup destroyed the life I envisioned for us. For myself.

Her palms are on my cheeks, gripping me with a ferocity that lets me know I hurt her just as deeply, ruined her just as badly.

She whimpers as I suck her bottom lip and I swear when her fingernails dig into the base of my neck.

"Beau," she gasps as I palm her breast, wanting to feel every inch of her body. Memorize it all over again.

"Fuck," I mutter. Losing my patience with our positions, I stand and sweep Celine into my arms.

"Beau!" She shrieks but I hear the lightness in her tone. She holds on to me as I stride to her bedroom. Plant her in the center of the bed.

Reaching behind my head, I grip the neck of my shirt and pull it off.

Celine's eyes drink me in.

I don't have time to wonder if I'm enough for her. Surely, a Hollywood starlet has dated men who look a thousand times better than me. But right now, I don't care. Right now, I just want to kiss her again.

Moving toward the bed, I lean over her. I'm about to kiss her when her legs dart out, wrap around my waist, and pull me down.

I fall over her, and she laughs.

"Shit," I swear as I catch myself before I land on top of Celine. I shake my head, gazing down at the beauty I want to drown in. Caging her head in between my forearms, I lower my mouth and kiss her hard.

Then, her fucking phone rings.

TWELVE
CELINE

"IGNORE IT," I demand when Beau pulls back.

Whoever is calling is not more important than this moment. Beau hesitates before capturing my mouth again. My thighs grip his hips harder. I want to feel him against me, but he won't close the few inches that separate us.

My palms flatten against his back as I pull him closer and he deepens our kiss, slanting his mouth over mine and kissing me with a hunger I love. I want Beau to devour me and remind me of what we once shared.

My phone rings again and Beau breaks our connection. "Fuck," he mutters and grips the back of his neck. "You gonna get it?"

I sigh and swing my legs to the side of my bed. "If you really want me to."

He snorts. "It could be important."

I give him a look over my shoulder.

He runs a hand over his face. "I'm sorry. I'm just used to... worrying. Is it Gran, is it Bea, is it one of the guys from my unit..." At the pain in his voice, I stand and move toward the kitchen for my phone.

"I get it," I tell him over my shoulder. "And I admire you for it. But I don't have the same responsibilities you do."

"I know." His voice is quiet.

It's one of the things that pulled us apart back then. Beau always had so many people to worry about, feelings to consider. I made plans for my future for myself. I didn't need to think about my siblings' educations or how my family would manage without me. I knew they'd be fine and, even though I didn't go the traditional college route my parents advocated for, they ultimately wanted me to pursue my dreams.

While Beau's family is certainly supportive, it's no secret he's made sacrifices for their well-being. Once he turned eighteen, he became the legal guardian of his siblings, as per his parents' wishes. Although Gran continued to take on most of the parental responsibilities, Beau stepped up too. Hell, him enlisting essentially paid for Bea's art school. Not to mention, the benefits his siblings received as his dependents.

My phone rings for the third time and I sigh. Maybe it is important. I swipe it off the countertop and roll my eyes when I see the caller. "Stalker much?"

Charlie laughs through the line. "Been trying to get ahold of you."

"What's going on?"

"You busy?"

I glance at Beau who hovers in the doorframe. My stomach sinks when I see he put his shirt back on. I would have liked more time to explore the hard planes of his chest, the sexy ridges of his abs. "Yeah," I tell Charlie.

"You okay?"

"Yeah," I repeat. "I'm great."

Beau rolls his eyes from the doorframe and leans against it, crossing his arms over his chest. He watches me carefully and I know he's wondering who I'm talking to. I'd sure as hell be wondering if I was standing in his shoes and he was talking to a woman a minute after kissing me.

"I want to come visit." Charlie's request snaps me back to our conversation.

"Uh, what? When?"

"Next week. Look, I can tell you're distracted, and I have to go anyway. I'm between takes."

"Now?" I glance outside at the night sky.

"I'm in Australia, babe," he reminds me.

"Oh, right," I mutter, rubbing at my forehead. I used to know Charlie's schedule as well as my own but since I've been in Tennessee, things have been hectic. My mind has been *occupied*. I glance at my newfound distraction and note the tension in his shoulders, the tightness of his jaw. He's jealous.

"I'll send you my flight details once I'm confirmed," Charlie continues.

"Okay, well, next week—"

"Charlie!" I hear his name being called in the background.

"Gotta go, babe. See you soon. Can't fucking wait." He clicks off.

Sighing, I toss down my phone. I turn toward Beau.

"Your guy?" he asks.

I blow out a sigh. "It's not like that."

"Then what's it like?" His tone is standoffish, and I hate it because before Charlie's incessant phone calls I felt like Beau and I were moving forward. We were being more than normal.

"Charlie and I are…friends."

Beau arches an eyebrow, calling me out. He stalks toward me, his expression lined with anger, his eyes gleaming with hurt. When he reaches my side, he drops his hands to the kitchen island, spreads his fingers, and leans in. "*Just* friends, Cece?"

I roll my lips together, try to keep my cool. My sex life has always been my own business and I've never been embarrassed about my choices but having to tell Beau—Beau!—that I occasionally sleep with my oldest friend in Hollywood is a new level of awkward. It's equal parts mortifying and terrifying. "We're friends with benefits. But friends first."

Beau's eyes shudder closed and his jaw ticks. He takes a deep breath.

"You can't pretend like you haven't been with anyone since us." I toss my arm wide.

Beau's eyes snap open, pin me in place. "While you're here, in Tennessee, I'm your fucking friend. I'm your provider of benefits. I'm whatever the hell you need me to be, Celine. While we're here, together, it's me and you. Not fucking Charlie"—he points to my phone—"or Thad."

"Thad?" I blurt out, incredulous. Why the hell would he think I had anything going on with Thad?

"Me," he murmurs, his palm pressing into his chest. "I'm your fucking guy."

A thrill rolls down my spine at the possessive gleam to his eyes, at the anger in his voice. I don't care that he's jealous. All I care is that he's reacting to me, giving me exactly what I want. *Him.*

A crack of thunder rumbles outside and it's like a bell going off. Beau and I lunge for each other, our mouths crashing, our hands gripping, clenching, pulling at each other's clothes.

Beau loses his shirt. Again.

I snap the button on his jeans, slipping my hands beneath the waistband and gripping his ass. I grind against him, and he swears.

He jerks down the zipper of my dress and it flows to the floor in a puddle I quickly step out of.

"Fuck," Beau swears, stepping back. His eyes drink me in, linger on each inch of my skin until I'm basking in his attention and burning for his touch. "You're the most gorgeous woman I've ever laid eyes on, Celine. Always have been."

His words tug at my chest, making me wish we didn't miss out on each other the past eight years. Wishing I made different decisions when I had the choices. I step into his space, and he wraps his arms around me.

Beau kisses me long and hard, his hands exploring my body with a reverent touch. My nipples are hard, digging into the lacy material of my bra, as I press myself against Beau. He unclasps my bra and drags the straps down my arms, kissing the column of my neck and the top of my left shoulder as the material falls away.

"Christ," he murmurs, cupping my right breast. I stare down, watch his hand test its weight, his fingers tweaking my nipple.

I gasp, arching into his touch. And then cry out, as his other hand slips between my legs. I widen my stance immediately, desperate for his touch. I haven't been with a man like this in too long. I'm needy, greedy, and desperate. But this is different; this is Beau.

When he pushes the slip of lace between my legs aside and drags a finger through my folds, I feel like I'm already going to slip over the edge.

"Damn, Cece. Baby, you're so wet," he mutters, his voice thick with desire.

"It's you," I tell him the truth. "No one's ever made me hot like you, Beau." My voice is half strangled with need.

"Fuck," he answers in a similar voice. His eyes screw closed and anguish twists his expression. Before I can ask what's wrong, he presses my lower back against the kitchen island and hitches one thigh up. Then his fingers part me and we both watch in fascination as Beau's fingers disappear inside me. The sounds of my arousal are loud. My panting is uncontrollable. And yet, I'm not embarrassed. I'm exhilarated. My thighs begin to shake and I claw at Beau's shoulders. He responds by dipping down to draw my naked breast into his mouth, his tongue swirling over my nipple.

"Oh God," I cry out, throwing my head back and bracing one palm against the kitchen island.

The edge is biting into my back. My legs feel like they're going to give out and still, Beau doesn't pull back. His thumb applies more pressure to my clit, and he massages it in time with his pulsing fingers, bringing me higher and higher.

My breasts are swollen, aching for his mouth. My nipples, desperate for his tongue. Heaviness gathers in my core, achy and needy and so fucking good.

My fingers twist in Beau's hair and he chuckles. Then, he surprises the hell out of me by dropping to his knees. The thigh he was holding is tossed over his shoulder. His eyes find mine and hold, gleaming wickedly.

"Fuck," I swear, the sight of him, on his knees before me, nearly my undoing.

Beau stares right at me, not even blinking, as he drags his nose up my center, followed by his tongue.

"Oh God. Beau!" I grip his hair harder.

His hand clamps the top of my thigh, keeping me open for him, while his other hand grips the back of my other knee. My knees feel like jelly and I stop pulling his hair to grip the edge of the island with both hands, if only to keep myself standing.

Beau swirls his tongue around my clit and licks me the way he kisses—fully and thoroughly.

The heat in my body expands, the ache intensifies, and then, I crest and fall.

"Beau, I'm coming. I'm coming for you!" I shout into my kitchen, my eyes closed, my head thrown back.

He grips my legs harder as his tongue lavishes my most sensitive part. As I come down from the most intense orgasm of my life, he lazily drags his tongue up my core two more times. So slow, I nearly come again, and my legs finally buckle.

I sink to the floor and Beau pulls me into his lap. He turns so his back rests against the island and my back rests against his chest.

"I...that...wow," I babble incoherently, the back of my head pressed against the base of his throat.

Undeterred, his fingers cup me, on top of my lacy panties he didn't need to remove to make me come so fucking hard, I'm still shaking. The pressure of his fingers makes me buck against him and he chuckles.

"I don't know what the future holds for us, Celine. But right now, we're us. You're mine. This belongs to me." He flexes his fingers again.

I tip my head back, look up at him. His eyes are a deep blue, swimming with emotion, dark with desire. His length is hard against my back, and I shift to reach for him but he grasps my wrist.

"Not tonight, baby. Tonight, you need to sleep, and I need to go."

I frown in confusion but Beau kisses it off my lips.

"Tonight was already more than I hoped it could be," he whispers.

I find his lips again and kiss him hard, tasting myself on his tongue. His hands lift to my breasts and touch me softly, longingly. "Beau," I murmur, my tone filled with want.

"I know, sweet Cece. Next time," he promises, brushing my hair back from my face. "Come on." He helps me stand and then, swings me into his arms.

"Beau!" I laugh. "I can walk."

"Humor me, Cece. It's been a long time since I've been able to care for you."

"Yeah. And who cares for you?"

At my question, sadness fills Beau's eyes but he blinks it away. He settles me in the center of my bed and moves into the bathroom. I hear the faucet run, then he comes back with a washcloth and cleans me up.

I shiver from his touch and a memory. Our first time

together. Making love in his bedroom at Gran's house. The way he held me afterwards, pressing kisses along my hairline.

I catch his wrist until he looks at me. "Tonight," I say, my voice husky, yet insistent. "Beau, this means something."

"I know, Celine." He leans forward and kisses me once. "It means everything." He pulls away and tugs my duvet up and over my shoulders. "Sleep, baby."

"Stay with me," I say, loving the way my sheets feel against my naked body. When was the last time I slept naked?

Beau smiles. "Soon," he promises. "I'll lock up and call you in the morning." His fingers brush over my cheek. "Set the alarm on your phone."

"I will."

"Good night, Cece."

"Good night, Beau." My eyes are already closing. The delicious orgasm Beau gave me was my last straw. That release, coupled with the stress of today, the intensity of filming, the excitement of tonight, crashes down on me.

I hear the front door close and then, I sleep more soundly than I have in years.

THIRTEEN
BEAU

THE IED ECHOES *in my head, rattling my brains and churning my stomach. Sand explodes, little particles that somehow end up everywhere. Stuck under the collar of my T-shirt, coating my skin in a film. My teeth grind together as my senses sharpen.*

Rein it in, Turner. Bury that shit.

I focus, looking at the devastation, the fucking wreckage and pillage, with a cold eye. No, not cold. Strategic. If I react emotionally now, I could get us killed.

"Incoming!" *Ramirez shouts.*

We take cover and when the bomb detonates, it shakes the fucking ground like an earthquake. I used to be scared of them, but that was before. Before I tasted true fear.

"Roberts is hit," *Ramirez hollers.*

I move over to Roberts, crouch beside him. Take his hand in mine and squeeze as blood sprays from his severed arm, gurgles up from the base of his throat. The medic, Samson, is trying to stop the bleeding but—he shakes his head. It's no use. It's too late. It's fucking over.

"Tell her I love her," *Roberts wheezes, his eyes blown with panic for several seconds until acceptance fills them. He knows he's dying.*

He knows he won't see his wife again. Or meet his baby girl. "Tell my girls I love 'em."

I grip his hand tightly. "Swear it, brother. I'll—"

"He's gone," Samson cuts me off.

Roberts's eyes are empty. He's gone.

"We gotta move. Move, move," Ramirez chants.

But I can't leave Roberts. I can't leave anyone. Heaving him up with a strength I didn't think I possessed, I fall into line. The remainder of our team moves out, having inflicted a hell of a lot less damage than the hits we took.

Gunfire surrounds us. A staccato of shots fire, sprays of bullets. My neck is so fucking itchy but when I scratch it, blood fills my palm.

"What the fuck?" I scrub harder at my neckline and watch in horror as the blood spreads, soaking through the collar and dripping down my shirt.

Now, Ramirez is gone.

"Ramirez!" I scream, but I can't see him anywhere.

I can't see anyone. Sand kicks up, swirling around me like a twister. My eyes burn, blinding me to everything except the grainy particles and the blazing heat.

"Celine!" Her name cuts the air like a foghorn. A warning, a plea, a fucking need. "Celine!"

The sand spins faster, catching me in its center. I watch in horror as my fingertips begin to fade, turning into grains of sand. The blood of my shirt spreads downward, covering me. My arms begin to disappear.

"Anyone!" I'm nearly crying now, begging for—what? Help? Love?

My body breaks apart and I disappear, nothing more than dust and blood. Part of the wreckage I inadvertently caused. Gone.

"Fuck!" I bolt straight up in bed.

I claw at the neckline of my shirt, gasping when I feel wetness, then nearly weeping in relief when I note it's sweat. I tug off the shirt and hurl it into the corner of my room.

My breathing is ragged; my chest too fucking tight. I can't suck in air quick enough and panic begins to build in my chest, assault my mind. I made the call to make a right that night. If we'd turned left instead, would we have hit an IED? Would we have become an easy target?

Would Roberts have died? Would we have lost Ramirez?

Guilt sticks to the walls of my stomach, twisting it so painfully, I catapult from bed and race to the bathroom. I throw up, my body heaving, as more sweat gathers on my forehead.

"Fuck," I mutter again. I rinse out my mouth, brush my teeth, gargle some mouthwash. Still the taste of shame and sand persists. I take a pill.

Rubbing my eyes, I note the time: 3:42 AM. I should sleep.

Yeah fucking right. Sleep won't come tonight.

Instead, I collapse on the couch and turn on mindless television. I close my eyes and allow myself to think of all the people I've let down.

Roberts and Ramirez. My brothers and Bea. Celine.

Celine fills my head. Her vanilla scent and easy laughter. The moans she makes and the feel of her hands on my back. The press of her heat against me, the sexy swell of her ass.

Celine who has a man on the side. Is it me? Or the other chump?

And what the fuck am I supposed to do with this knowledge? I can't share her. I won't. She needs to be mine or nothing at all. Because any alternative would kill me and I'm already bleeding out.

SLEEP NEVER COMES. Big fucking shocker.

I'm lagging when I make it to morning practice. The Honeycomb is mostly silent. I only see two of the regular juniors, Stanley and Jenkins, as I move toward the locker room.

"Ready for Chicago?" Stanley calls out.

"Yep," I reply, my tone curt, my head pounding.

The last thing I want to do right now is play hockey. Or see the guys on my team. More guys I'm going to let down if I don't get my head right, if I don't get my shit together.

But man, I'm tired. And terrified.

Did I fuck everything up last night with Celine? Can I do this with her when my mind is fragmenting in different directions?

"Yo," River greets me when I step to my locker.

I flip my chin at him.

He snickers, as if he knows the reason for my piss-poor attitude, and the sound of his laughter grates. Patton doesn't know shit. I don't know his story, but I'd bet my fucking life it isn't nearly as messed up and twisted as mine.

I change for practice and get onto the ice before anyone else can flip me their shit. Today, I'm not in the mood for it. Today, I'm not in the mood for anything. I just need to get through practice.

We run through a series of drills. I let four pucks slip past me in the first set.

Devon whistles. "Wake the fuck up, Turner."

I ignore him but my shoulders tense.

Coach Merrick regroups us, and we do another series of drills.

My head is foggy, my body is heavy. I'm crashing, my exhaustion from last night creeping in. I can't find a surge of adrenaline to see me through practice because I used it all last night. First, during my fucking nightmare and then afterwards, trying to talk myself through the paralyzing anxiety and gripping mental doubt.

Barnes takes a shot on goal and scores.

"Yo! You wanna try making a save today?" Patton taunts me.

"Fuck off," I holler back.

The arena falls quiet.

Coach Merrick's head swivels in my direction. "Get your head in this practice, Turner. Or get out of goal."

He throws out the ultimatum and I realize how badly I'm fucking up. Because if I'm being honest, my head hasn't been fully in any practice or game for weeks. Since Celine showed up in town and everything I've spent years burying came back to bite me in the ass.

"I'm fine," I say, mostly to convince myself.

Merrick nods. Devon fixes me with a steely gaze. Patton fucking smirks.

Practice resumes and I manage a few saves. A few decent plays. With only two minutes left, Damien Barnes takes an easy shot on goal and I fucking miss it. I don't even get a piece of the puck before it drops neatly into the right pocket.

Merrick blows his whistle. "What the hell was that, Turner? You gotta at least try." He gestures to the guys. "Line up. We're all taking shots."

I groan, knowing I deserve this punishment for my lackluster performance. The team lines up and come at me, one by one, taking shots.

Captain D'Amico, from my old unit, appears in my head. His voice rattles my eardrums. His Staten Island accent and no-nonsense demeanor. "You're a family. Family steps up for each other. Family protects each other. Loyalty. Commitment. The ability to do what needs to be done for each other, even if you wouldn't do it for your fucking self. Step up. That's what I expect from each of you."

Except I'm failing. I'm failing this team just like I failed the last one.

I miss five shots in a row.

Merrick's whistle cuts the air. "That's it." He fixes me a

look of pure disappointment and I know that Coaches Merrick and Scotch are going to call me into their office this week to ask me what the fuck is going on.

What am I going to say? I'm having nightmares like a goddamn toddler?

"No sleep last night?" Patton taunts.

"Shut it, Patton," Barnes warns, his voice low.

"Must be that actress, huh? She keep you up all night?" Patton doesn't fucking quit.

I spin on him, grip the front of his jersey and have him pinned up against the glass in a matter of seconds.

Patton's eyes widen for a beat but then, he stares back at me. His eyes flat, devoid of emotion. What the hell is wrong with this guy? Does he want to get fucking beat? He doesn't look scared. He doesn't even look angry. He almost looks... relieved.

"Do it," he sneers, as if begging me to punch him. When I don't move, he jeers, "Her pussy still as tight as you—"

The crack of his cheekbone hitting my knuckles rings in my ears. Before I can get another hit in, Brawler's got me planted against the glass, my cheek cutting into the hard plastic.

"What the fuck is going on with you?" Brawler's voice is low, collected.

And that pisses me off. Why is everyone so calm and in control? Why, when I feel like I'm splitting at the seams, is everyone else so fucking fine? Everything unravels, my thoughts, my emotions, *me*.

Images from the desert mix with the ice rink. Hot and cold. Heat and ice. Pain and disappointment.

I'm letting them all down.

Bury your fucking shit, Turner.

But I can't. The harder I try to push it down, the faster it comes up.

Anguished cries. Ramirez's wheezing. The blood—so

much goddamned blood. And sand. Burning heat and bright lights.

Brawler spins me around and the back of my head collides with the glass.

"I asked you a fucking question," he sneers, his eyes pinning me in place.

One minute, he's Axel Daire. Brown eyes and a fucking man bun. The next, he's every fucking failure of my life. I react. Without fucking thinking, I swing at Brawler and my entire body collides with the ice.

I HOLD the bag of frozen peas to my swollen eye and wince. Shit fucking hurts but it's my pride that's really wounded.

What the hell was I thinking, swinging at Axel? Getting into stupid shit with River?

I don't lash out like that. I don't make rash decisions. I calculate, I weigh options, I proceed accordingly. Right now, everything is out of control. I reach for wisps of the reality I've created, and it seems to disappear before my eyes. Like sand. Slipping through my fingers until there's nothing, no one, left.

I lean back on my couch and adjust the bag of peas.

My phone buzzes and I grope for it, hold it over my face.

Celine calling.

I don't answer. What the hell am I supposed to say to her? What I want from her and what I expect from her are two entirely different things that aren't lining up in my head. The best thing I can do right now is pull back, the way I should have from the beginning.

My phone chimes. I hold it up to glance at the email.

Sender: Coach Scotch

Subject: Meeting. My office. Monday at 9 AM.

Fuck. I drop my phone and close my good eye.

My teammates, mostly Cole, Devon, and Damien, have been blowing up my phone to check on me. Cole's called countless times and I know it's because he wants to know where my head is at before he confides in Bea. He won't keep today from my sister which means it's only a matter of time before my siblings descend on my quiet bachelor pad demanding answers I don't want to give.

I heave out a sigh.

Celine calling.

Ignore.

> COLE
>
> Pick up your phone, man. Bea's getting worried.

Jesus.

> BEA
>
> Beau, are you okay? I heard practice was rough today...

I toss my phone on the floor and listen to the sounds of my breathing.

Inhale. Exhale.

Bury it deep.

And finally, so long overdue my eyes burn, sleep comes.

It claims me. But still, relief doesn't follow.

Because sleep plunges me into a different world. One filled with horror and hurts. With howls and sand. One that leaves me riddled with anxiety and emptier than a black hole.

FOURTEEN
CELINE

I RUB my hands down the sides of my skirt as I stand on Gran's porch.

Maybe I should bail? Why am I even here?

I step back from the screen door and turn on my heel, pacing the length of the porch. In the corner, one of Gran's rockers sits and I plop down, staring at the front lawn.

Beau made me see stars and since then, radio silence. He hasn't answered my calls or texts; he didn't acknowledge the breakfast I had delivered to his place this morning.

Is it considered ghosting when I know where to find him? His truck is parked out front and I know he's inside, about to have dinner with his family.

But he didn't invite me. Bea did. And Bodhi. And Gran.

Shit. I blow out a deep breath. I could skip this right now, avoid the embarrassment and awkwardness it will entail, and take Thad up on his offer to grab a bite.

I don't move from my perch in the rocker.

What is wrong with me that I keep coming back for more rejection? For more of Beau's hot and cold antics? Is it because I'm clinging to the past? A past that hasn't existed for years?

Or because deep down, I know Beau is hurting just as much, maybe even more, than I am?

The screen door creaks as it opens and Bodhi steps onto the porch.

"Hey, Cece." He walks over and takes the rocker beside mine. He pushes back on the seat and laces his hands behind his head, casual. "You coming in?"

I fight a smile. "Thinking about it."

"What's the holdup?"

I give him a pointed look and he smirks.

"My brother's always been an ass," he remarks.

"Has Beau been…"

"What?"

"Off?" I ask hesitantly. Can I ask that when I've barely interacted with him in years?

Bodhi's expression sobers. "Since he got back," he admits slowly. "Beau…" He pauses again, considers his words. "He's got a lot going on." Bodhi taps his temple. "Too fucking much and sometimes, that gets in the way of things."

"He's ghosting me."

"He's not," Bodhi refutes. "He's overwhelmed."

"He used to be overwhelmed all the time," I say, recalling Beau's high school schedule. In addition to his schoolwork and hockey practices, he worked part time at a hardware store. He also went to all his siblings extracurriculars. Parent teacher conferences with Gran. He used to wrap birthday presents for Bea's friends and buzz Brody's hair short during baseball season. He did it fucking all and made it look easy.

"It's different now," Bodhi sighs. "Before, he had too many commitments, but he could mentally plan for them, make it work. Now, when he gets overwhelmed"—again, he taps his temple—"everything falls apart. He can't sleep. He can't eat. He can barely function."

"What happened in Afghanistan?" I ask, wanting to understand.

Bodhi shrugs. "He doesn't talk about it." His eyes wander to the screen door. "But it must've been fucking hell."

My heart breaks for Beau. Based on the changes I see in him, whatever went down destroyed part of his soul. And still, he tries to protect everyone, do right by his family, show up.

But I'd be lying if I said his not speaking to me after we shared what we shared hurts. I don't know if he means to reject me, but it feels like he doesn't care. That lack of concern, coming from him, lands differently. It makes me feel like I'm bleeding from the inside out and I haven't felt that way in a long time. Not since I accepted the role for *Midnight Moon* and Beau went overseas. A year went by before I realized I truly lost him. For good.

I shiver at the memory of those months. They were dark and I was alone and it *hurt*.

I don't want to hurt again but fuck, it hurts knowing that Beau's *hurting*.

I blow out a heavy sigh.

"You ready to come in?" Bodhi reads me better than he should.

I snort. "Yeah."

Bodhi stands and reaches out a hand to pull me up. Just as I stand, the screen door bangs open and Beau stalks outside, Cole on his heels.

"Talk to me, man," Cole says.

"I said to leave it alone." Beau whirls on his heel but halts when he sees me.

I do a double take when I notice his swollen eye. "Beau, what the hell happened to your face?"

Pure panic crosses his expression, and he laces his hands behind his head. "Fuck."

Cole gives me a sympathetic glance. His eyes snap back to Beau. "I'll be inside." Cole retreats into Gran's house.

Bodhi gives my hand a reassuring squeeze before

following Cole indoors. The screen door bangs closed followed by the storm door, ensuring that Beau's and my conversation won't be overheard.

That was definitely Cole. I can't remember a time when any of the Turner siblings gave Beau and me privacy to hash out our issues.

"What happened?" I ask again, pointing to his eye.

He shakes his head, his jaw tight. "Nothing. A misunderstanding."

"A mis —"

"I didn't think you were coming," he cuts me off, his voice hard. The warmth and want from a few nights ago is absent, as if it never happened.

"Gran invited me."

He snorts. "Of course she did."

"I'll leave if you want," I offer.

His eyes narrow. "Really? If I said I don't want you here, you'd go? Just like that."

I blow out a deep breath. "What's going on, Beau?"

He chuckles darkly. "That's what I thought."

"This isn't like you."

"Oh"—he tosses his arm out—"that's rich. Since when do you know me, Celine? It's been years since we were together. A few conversations, some breakfast deliveries, and a hookup doesn't change that."

I wince at the "hookup" comment because—is that all I am to him now? Was that all the other night was? A random, casual, meaningless encounter to pass the time?

"Bullshit," I call him out. "I know you, Beau. I've always known you. So, talk to me. What the hell is going on?"

Beau opens his mouth, as if to spit venom, but pauses as the door bangs opened again.

"Beau Michel Turner, stop making a damn spectacle on my front lawn." Gran's voice cuts the air. She holds the door open wider. "Celine, welcome, my dear. Please come in."

Gran's eyes hold mine with a steeliness I know better than to cross. It's determination mixed with grit. A testament to her ninety years on Earth coupled with all the children she raised, both hers and her grandchildren.

I clear my throat. "Yes, ma'am." I make my way toward the house and step inside as Beau stews on the front lawn.

A moment later, I hear his heavy footfalls behind us.

Gran effectively cut our conversation short and now, we're both at her dinner table. The Turner siblings and Cole's eyes are directed at their plates and an awkward silence descends over the table.

I should have bailed when I had the chance.

HALFWAY THROUGH DINNER, my eyes burn with unshed tears. Everyone, save for Gran, who is single-handedly carrying the conversation with some help from Bodhi and Bea, is uncomfortable. The tension is thick, lingering over the table like a thundercloud ready to burst.

My heart races, my hands feel clammy. Twice, I drop my fork. Both times, Cole winces. Both times, Beau ignores me.

What the hell happened to you?

I want to scream the words, but nothing comes out. Gran must sense it too because she doesn't put me on the spot with any of the direct questions she hurls at Bea.

"When's the grand opening of Humble Bee's again?" Gran asks.

Bea gives Gran an exasperated look. No doubt because Gran already knows the opening date of Bea's new store and is trying to fill the silence with safe conversation.

"November 18th," Bea replies.

"And your uncle and cousin are coming to it?" Gran waves her fork in Cole's direction.

Cole wipes his mouth with a napkin. "Yes, ma'am. Uncle Kirk can't wait to meet Bea, and Jamie wouldn't miss the opening."

"I look forward to meeting your uncle. Good man," Gran says with a nod of approval.

I glance at Beau who is doing his best to ignore me. In the past, this is the part where our eyes would meet, and we would have a silent conversation. With a few facial expressions, Beau would fill me in about Cole's family and I'd give a little nod of understanding.

He doesn't spare me a glance.

My tears come unbidden, burning behind my eyes and causing my throat to tighten.

Why won't you let me in?

Instead of hurling that at Beau's face, I politely excuse myself from the table. Bea gives me an empathetic look as I push back my chair and make my way to the bathroom.

I'm washing my hands when there's a soft knock on the door.

For a second, my heart swells with hope that it's Beau but when I open the door and see Bea, my shoulders slump.

"My brother's an idiot," Bea declares, pushing her way into the bathroom and closing the door behind her. She leans back against it, crossing her arms over her chest. Her expression is stern although her grey eyes are soft with understanding.

I plop down on the closed toilet lid and sigh. "I don't know why he's shutting me out. Not like we're best friends or anything but the last time we hung out..." I trail off, hoping Bea will read between the lines and not make me say it.

"He got too close," she says.

I narrow my eyes.

"He fucked up at practice yesterday too. Cole told me he got into it with a guy on his team. The biggest guy on his team. Swung at him."

I swear. "That explains his swollen eye."

"Yeah."

"But, that's so unlike Beau."

Bea shakes her head. "He's different now, Celine. He's... haunted by things that happened in Afghanistan. He won't open up to any of us about what happened. Cole's been trying to get him to talk to a therapist."

"The one that helped get Cole involved in the youth rehabilitation programs?"

"Yeah." Bea smiles. "But Cole's therapist has some contacts that deal specifically with PTSD. Beau won't go."

I sigh, not surprised. Beau's always been a protector. A provider. A man in control. The one who calls the shots. It would be tough for him to admit he needs help, never mind therapy.

"I wish he'd hear Cole out," I murmur.

"Me too," Bea sighs. "But I wanted to tell you, it's not you. The way he's acting, his behavior in general, it's not you."

I lift my eyebrow, calling her out.

Bea sighs again, throwing her hands in the air. "Fine. It is you. But only because he cares about you so damn much. This has been in the works for months. Beau's been withdrawing, keeping more to himself. He's different now. You coming home, it must have changed something for him because he's reacting. But I don't think that's a bad thing, Celine. I think it means he cares. It just sucks that you're on the receiving end of his shit while he sorts out his thoughts and feelings."

"He's been so hot and cold," I offer, tapping my fingers against my thighs. I fold my hands together to stop fidgeting and end up wringing my hands.

Bea's look turns sympathetic as she nods miserably. "I'm sorry. And I know this is super selfish but...don't give up on him. Not yet. I know he still cares about you."

It's my turn to sigh. "I care about him too, Bea. But I don't

know." I shake my head. "I don't even live here. All of this"—
I gesture around the space—"is temporary."

"I know," Bea whispers. "Just, for now, while you're here, please don't give up on my brother. You stand a better chance of getting through to him than the rest of us combined."

"Bea," I say slowly, "I'll do whatever it takes to help Beau. You know that. But I can't keep breaking my heart in the process."

"I know," Bea agrees. "You're right. Just, a little more time, Celine. Not yet," she pleads before I can say anything.

I nod in agreement.

My hands may feel shaky and my mind a mess of thoughts, but my heart still beats for Beau Turner. I'd never truly give up on him.

FIFTEEN
BEAU

I HATE that she's hurting. The pain in her eyes was agony to endure and yet, I put it there. I fucking hurt Celine.

I grip the back of my neck, pinching tightly.

"You should check on her," Bea murmurs, passing me in the hallway.

I ignore my sister, my eyes glued to the bathroom door Celine disappeared into. Is she crying? Does she hate me?

I hear the faucet turn on in the bathroom and I hesitate.

Isn't it better if she hates me? I have nothing to offer her. Nothing real to give.

Years ago, Celine left this town, left this life behind. She shed it easily and stepped into a new world. One brimming with glamour and excitement. One that allows her to fulfill her goddamn passion. She's an incredibly talented actress.

I pace in front of the bathroom door. If Gran saw me, she'd tsk that I'm wearing out her floor. It feels like I could grind away until I hit the subfloor and none of the shit in my head would be clear. Nothing makes any damn sense anymore.

Except I *see* Celine. The longing in her eyes for what was. The way she lit up when we went to The Rib Shack of all places. How easily she stepped back into this world, as if a part of her regrets leaving it in the first place.

Does she regret leaving me?

And the sounds she made the other night. The heat of her body, pressed up against mine. I bite my fist. I'll never get enough of her; it will never be enough. My desire for Celine is insatiable and I want all of her.

Even though she'd never want all of me.

Jesus, I need to get a fucking grip.

I stop in front of the bathroom door. Knock.

Celine pulls it open and fuck, she's gorgeous. And pissed. And *hurt*. Emotions emanate from her, crashing into me like a forcefield. She narrows her eyes when she sees me, standing straighter and staring me down.

I grip the sides of the doorframe, leaning forward, crowding her even though it's wrong. Everything about Celine and me is wrong. We used to make so much sense together and now—fuck, now I want to kiss the memory of me away. Fuck it out of her. Leave her with an imprint of the new version of me so she'll know better. After this, I'll never hurt her again.

Never make her fucking cry.

Not over my messed-up shit. Not over the shell of a man I've become. Because there's no chance in hell she'll want me again.

"What do you want?" she asks, her voice strong, her tone soft.

I step into the bathroom and Celine backs up. Her eyes flare, searching my face for a clue. *What is he thinking?* she wonders. *What is he going to do?*

I kick the bathroom door closed behind me. Reach for her hips.

"Beau."

I grip her, pull her flush against my frame.

Her breathing is ragged, indecision and want battling in her irises.

I hold her tighter, dip down. Let my mouth graze the shell of her ear.

She shivers and I almost let go. I shouldn't do this. I should walk away.

Laughter rings out in my mind. Yeah, right. I'm so far past that; I need a reason to go. I need to destroy everything, burn it all to the fucking ground, and then, when the option of her isn't tangible, when the chance of Celine is destroyed, I'll be forced to go.

"Wanna fuck you out of my system," I admit, my voice gravelly.

Her arms link over the tops of mine and she grips my biceps. "I don't want to fuck you like I want to throw you away," she replies, hinting that she knows what I'm up to.

I should be surprised but I'm not. Celine's always been too damn smart. Too damn good. Too damn everything.

But I can't concentrate on that now. Not with the scent of her filling my nostrils, the feel of her frustration vibrating under my palms, the bite in her tone I want to swallow.

"I do," I reply, turning my head.

Celine's eyes flash with a challenge right before my mouth descends on hers. When I kiss her, she responds, giving me her anger, her resentment, her *hurt*. And fuck, I want to take it.

So, I do. I kiss her hard until she rips her mouth from mine and glares.

"Talk to me, Beau."

"I want you, Celine." My voice is raspy, like I swallowed rocks.

She moves to reach for me but thinks better of it and that pisses me off. Frustrates me as much as it confuses me. I crowd her, advancing until her back hits the wall on the far side of the bathroom. Then, I angle her chin upward, drown in her dark eyes that spark with anger and bleed with hurt. Oh, but I note the hint of desire in their midst.

Celine's chest brushes my abdomen with every pant of breath and I close the space between us, pinning her to the wall. With her eyes on mine, I kiss her again. The space between us ignites. Her mouth is hot on mine. My lips are frantic on hers.

Our teeth clash as I press into her, and she arches against me. I grab a handful of her ass and she hitches her leg up, grinding against me. I grasp her thigh, my fingers digging into her skin. Her nails scrape at my upper back.

It's a passionate battle, a duel of wills.

Talk to me.

Give it to me.

My mind empties and the only thing left is the animalistic need I have to take her. To show her the savage I've become. So she'll know the truth. There's no fucking hope. There's no future.

There's nothing but this.

And this is gritty. And desperate. And fucked.

I pull on her hair, exposing her neck. My mouth glides down the column, kissing and nipping and making her hiss in my ear.

She pulls my shirt up and over my head, her nails scraping from the base of my back to my neck. Celine tosses my shirt on the floor and holds my eyes as she removes her blouse.

Fuck. My mouth waters at the sight of her perky breasts, just more than a handful, in a dusty rose, lace bra. I reach out, almost tentatively and palm one, my thumb pressing over the point of her nipple. I love that I can see the outline of her nipples through the fabric, love that she's as turned on as I am. I yank down the cup of her bra as my other hand slides between Celine's thighs. Her skirt bunches up around her waist and I almost grin when I note that her panties match her bra.

Sweet rose. Racy lace.

"Beau," she gasps, closing her eyes and letting her head fall back against the wall.

"Spread your legs," I demand, watching her face closely.

She does what I say. No hesitation in her expression. Her eyes don't even flutter open at the command in my tone. My cock's been hard since the second I stepped into the bathroom but now it feels like it's going to explode if it doesn't get inside Celine's hot body.

With the extra room, I pull her panties to the side and run my finger down her core. She presses her breast into my palm and I play with her nipple. Lowering my mouth to her neck, I suck, wanting to mark her as mine. Even if I can't truly have her, I want everyone to know that in the ways that matter—the desperate, yearning, complicated ways—she'll always be mine.

"Mine," I growl, reminding her of my declaration from the other night.

I plunge two fingers inside her wet pussy and she gasps. As I work her up, her hands drop to my jeans. She pops the button and pulls down the zipper in record time. Her hands push my jeans, along with my boxers, over my hips and down my legs. I don't bother to step out of them as I push against her.

When her hand wraps around my cock, she inhales sharply, dragging in a gulp of air.

"Fuck, baby," I murmur when she begins to work my shaft.

My fingers move faster, the sounds of her arousal, her panting, filling the bathroom. She tips her hips upward, giving me better access and I roll the pad of my thumb over her swollen clit, applying the extra friction she needs to send her over the edge.

"Oh God, Beau," she cries out, biting the top of my shoulder to muffle her noise.

Before she can come down from her orgasm, I'm pinning her to the wall. "Look at me," I demand.

She does.

"You on birth control?"

Celine nods.

"You want me bare?" Because fuck if I know where a condom is in this moment.

"Yes," she half sobs. Whether it's in desire or hurt at my callousness, I have no idea. And right now, I don't take the time to figure it out because I'm too far gone.

My only objective right now is to feel her pretty pussy clench around me. To know that I still got a piece of Celine, even if I'll never be good enough to claim all of her.

I grasp her ass and hitch her higher. With my hands wrapped around the backs of her upper thighs, I anchor her back to the wall and enter her. One sharp push and I'm rooted deep, swearing as she cries out.

I still for a second. Our eyes hold. And then, I fuck her like the angry, resentful, bitter man I've become. Hard, desperate, and unyielding.

Celine takes it, her eyes wild, her cheeks red. Her nails claw at my skin, her teeth rake over my shoulder, her fingers twist in my hair.

She comes a second time and only then do I let myself go, quickening the pace until I'm clinging to the edges of reality. At the last second, I pull out, grab Gran's embroidered hand towel, and spill my seed into the fabric.

Celine's breathing is ragged as she watches me. Her expression is unreadable, lined with too many emotions to fully understand.

Anger and hurt. Pity and guilt. Worry and want.

I avert my gaze. My fingers tremble and I hide them in the

towel as a tidal wave of shame crashes down on me. My head buzzes and my stomach churns.

What have I done?

I can't meet her eyes; I can't look up.

How could I take Celine against the wall in Gran's bathroom like she's nothing more than a casual fuck?

How the hell could I put her in this position when us fucking changes nothing. Absolutely nothing.

And fucking everything.

Hanging my head, I stare at her open-toed sandals. The vibrant green polish on her toenails makes me want to sob.

I clear my throat.

Rein it in. Bury that shit.

I pass Celine a clean towel from under the sink and pull up my jeans.

"Clean up," I tell her. "Then, I'll take you home."

She sucks in a breath, her eyes wide as they fly over my face. Then, she turns away, her shoulders slumped with the shame I feel coursing through my veins like heroin.

I give her a moment to pull herself together. Then, I take both of our towels, crumple them in my hand, and lead her out of Gran's house. We take the back door, luckily avoiding my family members.

I drive to Celine's house and the silence stretches between us. So loud, it's like being at *The Burnt Clovers* concert.

I fucked up big time and yet, what the hell do I say? Sorry is inadequate and I can't offer much more than that. I stay silent and when I pull up to Celine's place, she vaults herself from the truck and slams the door closed.

There's no closure. Nothing's resolved.

I guess she hates me now.

Part of me hopes she does since that was the intent.

Part of me hopes she doesn't because Celine's hate will destroy me. And I'll finally get what I deserve.

I FEEL like shit when I wake up on Monday morning.

I drag my ass out of bed at 4 AM and go through the motions. I chug a smoothie, get ready for a morning skate, and try to get my head on straight.

But Celine's eyes, bleeding with hurt, gut me.

What the fuck was I thinking treating her so crassly? So crudely? Like I don't give a shit at all.

Do you? My conscience taunts me. *Isn't it better this way? Let her hate you; it's not like she'd ever love you again.*

I scrub a hand over my face. Drive my ass to the The Honeycomb. Ignore the shit swirling in my stomach, swallow back the guilt that crawls up my throat.

Bury it, Turner.

I try. I really fucking do.

But right before I take the ice, Celine sends me a text.

CELINE

> Talk to me. Please, Beau. I can't stand the way things are between us.

Her message rips me up and I skate onto the ice, hoping to clear my head. Two hours later, I don't feel any better. The fact that hockey couldn't put me in a better headspace is worrying. So is the meeting I have with Coach Scotch.

I take a shower after practice, trying to quell the negative thoughts and natural nerves rattling around my head.

Is Scotch going to bench me? Force me to do some mandatory therapy shit? Make me do extra workouts?

The not knowing is worse than the knowing. I need to get through my meeting with Scotch and then, I'll rally. I'll make a plan; I'll mentally prepare.

I towel off and dress for my meeting.

It's fine. Get your head right. One step at a time.

When I go to Scotch's office, he's not there. Instead, a Post-it is stuck to the door.

Beau,

Meet in the weight room. Get ready to work.

- Coach

Fuck. I groan, raking a hand through my hair.

Is Coach going to put me through another workout when we have a game tomorrow? We're flying to Toronto tonight.

Sighing, I make my way to the weight room. When I enter, I'm surprised to see Devon and Axel.

"What are you doing here?" I ask.

"They're here for you," Coach Scotch replies, coming around a corner with a set of battle ropes. He gestures to a corner where some boxing gloves and headgear sit.

I frown.

"You clearly wanna throw punches," Scotch says, dropping the battle ropes. "You wanna go head-to-head with Daire?"

Axel winks at me, cocky motherfucker. Devon smirks.

"Now's your chance," Scotch explains.

"What?" I ask, not following. "You want me to…box with Axel?"

"I want you to work out whatever the hell is going on in your head so you can get your mind where it's supposed to be." Scotch crosses his arms over his chest.

"On hockey," I fill in the obvious blank.

"Among other things." Coach surprises the hell out of me.

My eyes snap to his.

Scotch sighs. "I know your stuff is bigger than this." He points to the makeshift ring in the corner. "This is temporary; I know that. But you need a shove to get moving in a new direction and Daire's gonna be that push." He tips his head toward the gloves. "Suit up, gentlemen."

Daire cracks his knuckles. Devon fucking laughs.

"You're serious?" I question.

"I realize this is unorthodox and I'm crossing some lines here, but Daire is up for it. Consider it 'team-building.'" He air quotes. "There's nothing explicitly stated in your contract against activities that bolster team bonding. Get in the fucking ring and start working through your shit, Turner," Coach demands. He points between us. "And the two of you better bring your best on the ice tomorrow night. No head shots, no kidney hits. Keep it clean. We have a game and I need your head in it, Beau."

Shit. He's serious. I do as Coach says, taking off my hoodie and wrapping my hands before donning boxing gloves. I pull the headgear on and step into the center of the marked off mats. Bouncing from one foot to the other, I attempt to warm up.

"That's cute," Axel says, his expression set. He's the fucking Brawler and right now, he's living up to his nickname. He cracks his neck and I wince. "You ready for me, Turner?"

At his taunt, I narrow my eyes.

Rein it in.

I tap my gloves, and my thoughts fly from my mind. Instead, I let the anger living in my veins flow freely. "Bring it, Daire," I sneer.

"I'm setting a timer for three minutes. Don't break anything," Coach warns, his tone deceptively casual.

Devon inserts mouthguards into Daire's and my mouths. "Wouldn't want to ruin your smiles."

Then, Coach starts the clock and Daire and I jostle around each other.

Daire lands a jab, cutting me across the chin. I stagger back and swear. Biting down on my mouthguard, I focus on Axel. No way in hell am I going down.

Daire jabs and I block it, but he nails me with a cross. I retaliate, my blood pounding in my eardrums. Adrenaline and anger mix, propelling me forward.

Axel and I go at it, swinging and blocking. Weaving and crossing. He pushes me, driving my anger. When he lands a hook to my left side, I throw a wild jab that strikes him in the chest.

Daire fucking laughs and the sound infuriates me. I lose my cool. My ability to remain in control slips and I let loose with a combination of jabs, crosses, and hooks that are more desperate than logical.

Axel takes it, blocking some, missing others. But he doesn't back down and his willingness to step to me encourages me to keep moving. My mind clears for the first time in weeks. The constant worry, the paralyzing anxiety, the crippling fear floats away.

All I'm left with is anger and resentment and regret. I channel it all and hurl it at Axel.

Jab, jab, cross. Double hook, uppercut. Cross, jab, hook.

The bell sounds but we don't stop. Instead, Axel spits out his mouthguard.

"Come at me, motherfucker," he sneers. "Give me your shit."

I lose my mouthguard too. "Fuck off," I tell him. He blocks my punch and I crack, letting out a howl and rushing him.

I tackle Axel to the mat, and he goes down like a tree trunk. Surprise flares in his irises but in the next moment, he's flipped me onto my back. I block his punch and we clinch, both of us swearing, as our boxing turns into wrestling.

Scotch and Devon don't intervene.

"Where the fuck is your head at?" Daire wheezes.

Emotion rushes through me at his question. Bile crawls up my throat. I have the urge to fucking sob which is stupid. And impractical. And the opposite of survival.

I knee him and he punches me.

We break apart, both of us panting.

"What are you scared of?" Daire stares right at me, his chin red, his eyes solemn.

"Not living," I wheeze out, giving him the truth.

He shakes his head. "We're all gonna die eventually, Turner. I doubt your time's up today. What are you scared of?"

"Not dying," I spit out, gasping for air. Death has never been my fear. "I'm scared of not *living*. Of squandering the chance I got."

Recognition blazes through Axel's eyes as he understands what I'm saying. "Yeah? You think pushing Celine away is living?"

I glare at him, knowing Cole must've fed him some information about my personal life.

"You don't fucking get it."

"Try me," Axel snaps.

I force myself to stand, smack my glove against my chest. "You think Celine Hernandez wants to be with this?" I hit myself again. "I'm a fucking shell, Daire. Nothing like the man I was."

"No," he agrees, even though he didn't know me back then. "You're better now."

I give him an incredulous look. Shaking off my gloves, my wrapped hands curl into fists. Part of me wants to hit him now.

"You are," he insists, standing. "Because you know what's at stake. You've tasted death. Grief. Sorrow. Loss." He punctuates each word with a shove to my shoulder. "You know better than to squander the chance you fucking got. Your biggest fear? You're already living it by not fucking living, you dumbass." With that he taps the side of my headgear with his glove and walks out of the ring.

I watch him go, hating that he made sense.

"That's some tough love shit right there," Devon remarks. "You can tell he's a dad, huh?"

Coach Scotch tips his head toward the weight room door and Devon follows Daire.

Coach looks at me. "You want to talk?"

I shake my head, still breathing heavily.

Coach nods. "Welcome to your first therapy session."

"Fucking Cole." I close my eyes, knowing Cole must've also told Coach that I'm resistant to the therapy shit he keeps bringing up.

Scotch smiles. "See you on the plane, Turner. Your next session is Thursday morning."

"We have a game Wednesday," I remind him.

"I know," he says before exiting the weight room.

I sink to the mat and lie down, stare up at the ceiling. What the hell was that?

And why do I feel a little bit better than when I woke up this morning?

SIXTEEN
CELINE

BEAU

Can I come over?

I HUFF when I see his message. Tossing down my phone, I pad to the kitchen and pour myself a glass of sparkling water.

The nerve of this man! He fucks me hard against a wall in his grandmother's house, disappears for three days—fine, I know he had a game, but *still*—and now, sends me a text?

Anger coupled with hurt shoots down my spine as I glare at my phone like it's offended me. I'm not replying to his message.

As if on cue, my phone rings.

Damn Beau Turner.

I move back across my kitchen and pick up the phone. When I read his name on the screen, my irritation skyrockets but so does my curiosity. I cave.

"Hello?"

"I need to see you."

"Really?"

"I'm sorry for how I treated you, Celine," Beau says,

surprising me. "And I want to say that to your face, so you'll know I mean it."

I pull the phone away from my ear and take a deep breath. Beau's behavior, hot and cold, back and forth, is giving me whiplash. "I had a really long day shooting," I say. It's the truth and I'm not sure if I'm in the right head space to deal with his flip-flopping emotions tonight.

"Please." His voice cracks on the word. Remorse bleeds through his tone.

My heart splinters a little. "Fine."

"Thank you," he sighs in relief. "I'll be there in ten. Do you need anything?"

I roll my eyes. "No." I hang up the phone.

I glance around my place. Everything is neat and tidy. Just like my life until I came back to Tennessee and Beau rolled through it like a blizzard. Blasts of arctic cold followed by moments of perfect tranquility and beauty.

I pace around the space, my eyes glued to the front window, waiting for the beams of his headlights. The chemistry between Beau and me is still there, perhaps even more now. He lights my body up just by being in the same breathing space.

But he didn't used to be so moody. I used to talk to him about everything. Maybe it's me? Maybe I didn't manage my expectations. How could the Beau Turner I loved in high school be the same Beau Turner who just pulled into my driveway? This man has gone to war, to hell and back. This version is struggling. He makes cutting remarks and gives blank expressions when the guy I fell in love with wore his heart on his sleeve. I watch Beau walk toward my front door and ascend the porch steps. I wait for his knock.

Then, I take a deep breath and steel my spine. I need to confront *this* Beau. I need to set boundaries. I need to let him know that he can't keep disappearing.

I pull the door open.

His eyes meet mine and the fact that he looks awful, exhausted, *hurting*, doesn't offer even a sliver of satisfaction. Instead, I feel terrible that he's struggling this much.

"Come in," I command.

He steps inside, plunges his hands into his pockets, and looks around my place. His gaze is wary when it meets mine. Dark circles are stamped beneath his slate-colored eyes, and he hasn't shaved in a few days. The prickly coating of his beard makes him look older. Sadder somehow.

"Celine…" His voice breaks. "I'm so fucking sorry."

"Thank you," I reply, accepting his apology because I know he means it. I turn on my heel and Beau follows. He sits down at the kitchen island while I brew us peach tea.

I arrange some baked goods one of my costars left in my trailer today onto a little dish and set it before Beau.

He gives me a look. "Still got a sweet tooth?"

I nod. "But don't tell Paulo. I downplay it."

Beau's eyebrows dip. "Paulo?"

"My trainer. He's been sending me workouts, that I've been doing. But in LA, he's pushing my ass at 6 AM."

"Damn," Beau mutters, swiping a pastry and taking a bite.

"It's not that different than hockey mornings." I shrug, helping myself to a custard doughnut I've been thinking about since I saw the sweet treats this morning. I take a bite and close my eyes, savoring the sugar rush.

Silence stretches between us. I stare at Beau, waiting for him to say something. This time, I'm not making it easier for him.

Beau clears his throat. "You have no idea how fucking sorry I am for the shit I've been pulling."

I blink.

"The other day, at Gran's…that was way out of line. I never should have spoken to you that way. I never should have pushed you away like that."

I take another bite of my doughnut, lick the powdered sugar off my lips.

Beau sighs. "Celine, I'm fucking sorry."

"You should be, Beau," I spit out. His apology, while appreciated, only ratchets up my emotions. My eyes fill with tears that I frantically blink away. "You're playing mind games with me. Besides being confusing as hell, it's hurtful."

Regret pours from Beau's expression like an open tap. For the first time since I've returned to Knoxville, he's the guy I remember. He's wearing his heart on his sleeve, showing me his remorse. "I fucked up, Celine. I know it. But I'm going to make it up to you. You have no idea how much I miss you. How much I think of you. Celine, it's always been you."

"You have a strange way of showing it. You disappear from my life for nearly a decade—"

"You didn't reach out either."

"And then, you're all, while we're in Tennessee, I'm your guy. Which I thought meant something real, you know? It kills me that I can't read you. That I don't understand you. That it's obvious you're struggling—"

He flinches but I continue.

"And you won't let me in. Unless you want to fuck—"

He shakes his head, his discomfort obvious.

"But you won't give me anything real to work with. I keep trying to do little, silly things to let you know I'm thinking of you. That I want you in my life. Sending you breakfast or texting you in the middle of the day, whatever. But you…you use me and then push me away."

"I don't mean to, Celine. Believe me. When we're together, everything in my head finally goes silent. Being with you cuts all the noise, but afterwards, it fucks with me. I feel too much when I'm with you. It brings back the past and not all of that past is good."

I frown. "From high school?"

"From Afghanistan," he admits.

"What happened, Beau?"

"The worst things you can ever imagine," he says slowly, echoes of horror shading his eyes. "I'm working through... shit. But I never should have taken that out on you. The things I feel for you, Celine..." His voice breaks. "And if that ever happened to you...if I ever put you in a dangerous position..." He trails off again. Then, his eyes meet mine and hold. A decisiveness that sends a thrill through me sparks in his gaze. "Give me a shot, Celine."

"Why?" I ask, straightening. My arms cross over my chest defensively. Even though Beau is saying words I want to hear, "I don't trust you."

His mouth twists. "I know," he agrees. "I haven't given you a reason to. But let me show you. Give me a chance to prove to you that my feelings, the way I miss you, it's real. It matters. You matter so fucking much to me. Just, give me a chance. Day by day, moment by moment, let's enjoy what we have."

"For as long as we have it?" I question. "After the holidays, I'm heading back to LA."

"I know." Beau's jaw is set now. "But until New Year's, you're here."

I weigh his words. While I can tell he's truly sorry for the hot-and-cold shit he's been flipping my way, I can't see how things are going to miraculously improve in a few months.

"You're giving me something to work toward, Celine. Don't you see? You being here, it's changing things for me. And yeah, it's hard and scary. I've been burying things for a long-ass time. But I want to get better, Cece. And you're giving me the motivation I need to do that. I need you, Celine."

I meet Beau's eyes, note the sincerity swimming in them. "I want to trust you, Beau."

"Then give me a chance to prove to you that you can. That I can be worthy of you again."

Slowly, I nod in agreement. I want what he's offering more than he understands. But will he follow through? Are "we" even a possibility anymore? Or just an echo of the past?

Beau reaches for my hand and grips it. Sparks shoot down my fingers, little flares of desire skate over my skin. I close my eyes and sigh. "You really hurt me, Beau. And it's not the first time."

He's quiet, listening to the sounds of our mingled breathing.

I open my eyes. "And I've hurt you."

He averts his gaze.

I sigh. "What's changed?"

"Celine, please." His eyes snap back to mine.

"I don't have infinite chances to give," I warn him.

"I get it, Cece. I really do."

I bite my bottom lip but tip my head in his direction.

Whatever Beau and I are, it's confusing. And difficult. Yet, I want it more than anything else in the world. Even if I have to fight for it. Fight for him.

SEVENTEEN
BEAU

"HOW'S IT GOING, BEAU?" Thad Stevens greets me as I try to get on set to surprise Celine. I contacted her assistant earlier who assured me I'd have no problem but without Celine to sign me in, I've been standing here, holding a smoothie and some salads, for fifteen minutes.

Luckily, Thad passed by and got me through security.

"It's going." I lift the smoothie and salad bag higher. "You hungry?" Thank God I grabbed extra salads.

Thad smacks my back. "Nah, I'm good. But thanks for the offer, man. This is Celine's trailer." He points to the door. "She should be back in the next fifteen minutes or so. You want to surprise her, or should I give her a heads-up?"

I grin, liking Thad's easy vibe. "I'll surprise her."

"Sweet. See you later." Thad lopes off.

I enter Celine's trailer and glance around, surprised by how big and neat it is inside. I know it's a space for her to unwind and relax in between scenes but I didn't expect it to be so...well, luxurious.

I place her lunch down on a little dinette table and take a seat. It's quiet in here and for the first time since we ended things, I think about Celine's life in a different light.

The endless travel, hopping from one place to the next, always having to be on. Smile, stand straight, wave, sign autographs. Look the part, take the interview, memorize the lines.

From an outside perspective, her life seems glamorous and fulfilling. But inside this trailer, I sense the loneliness that rounds out her day-to-day routine.

The door to the trailer opens and I straighten.

"Yes. We'll touch up makeup and then—" Celine's voice trails off as she sees me. She grins. "Beau! What are you doing here?"

Behind Celine, a petite woman with a clipboard pauses.

I point to the table. "I brought you ladies lunch."

The woman winces. "Sorry, Beau! I forgot to clear your name with security." Ah, so it is her assistant, Mellie.

"That's all right." I wave a hand. I can't imagine how busy her day-to-day is if she's in charge of keeping track of Celine's schedule, engagements, and commitments.

Celine gives Mellie an understanding smile. "Are you hungry?"

Mellie shakes her head. "No, I'm good. I'll leave you two to it. Cece, I'll be back when it's time to touch up your makeup."

"Thanks." Celine takes the seat across from mine.

Mellie excuses herself from the trailer.

I push the bag closer to Celine.

She beams at me. "This is a nice surprise. You didn't have to bring me lunch." She pulls out the three salads. "Ooh, I love a southwestern chicken salad!" She pushes the Mediterranean one in my direction and shoves the plain garden salad off to the side.

I snort and pop the lid, picking up a plastic fork. "How's your day been?"

Celine shrugs. "So far, so good. This movie is really coming together. I love playing Carley, my character. She's so…real, you know? The stress she's under, the moving parts she's navigating, the family pressures, it's all relatable. And complicated. It's pushing me to expand and be more open to Carley's struggles."

"I'm sure you're doing an incredible job."

Celine shrugs and takes a gulp of her smoothie. "I hope so. I'd really like to play more roles like Carley and distance myself from Magdalena. Not that I didn't love playing her, but I don't want to be pigeonholed for fantasy films."

I nod, thinking that over. "Makes sense. If you win an Oscar…"

Celine laughs and flashes her hand, crossing her fingers. "From your lips to God's ears, Beau. How's your day?"

"Good. I had an early skate, followed by a lift. I'm sparring this afternoon wi—"

"Sparring? Isn't that…I don't know, prohibited by your contract or something?"

I snort, thinking of Coach Scotch. "Not when your coach requires it."

Celine's eyes widen.

I shrug. "Coach is considering it therapy. A chance for me to work out some of the shit up here." I tap my temple. "He's set some boundaries but…it seems to be helping."

Celine clears her throat, her eyes shadowed with worry. "I'm glad to hear that but have you ever considered speaking with someone? Like a professional?"

"You sound like Cole."

"He's a smart guy."

I shrug. "I'll take it under advisement but for now, I like the sparring."

Celine nods.

"I'm flying out tomorrow morning. We have an away game in Dallas."

"Oh." Celine crumples a napkin in her hand and leans back in her seat.

"But our Friday game is home. Want to come and get drinks with my team afterwards?"

Celine gasps, surprise lining her face. "You want to introduce me to your team?"

"Very much."

She smiles. "Okay. I'd like that. And, next weekend, you can meet my friend Charlie."

"Charlie?" My voice holds an edge.

Celine notices because she sucks in a breath. "He's coming to visit for the weekend."

"To see you?"

She nods. "I'd like you to meet him."

Jealousy swirls in my gut but what the hell am I going to say? I have no right to feel the way I do. If anything, I should be grateful Celine has such a solid friend. Even if he wants more than friendship with her. I clear my throat. "Can't wait."

"Yay!" she exclaims with extra enthusiasm. "Maybe we can do dinner one night?"

"Sure."

"I'm filming Sunday morning and Charlie is going to be on set. You can join him if you'd like."

"Oh, I'll be here," I confirm, hating the idea of him showing up for her without me. Hating that for the past seven years, he showed up when I didn't.

"Then it's settled." Celine looks genuinely pleased at the weekend plans.

I force a grin and shove some salad into my mouth.

How the hell am I supposed to win back my girl when I'm competing with famous actor Charlie Ryerson? There's no doubt in my mind that he carries a torch for Celine. That he has serious feelings for her.

Feelings I don't want to consider when my feelings for Celine are complicated and confusing. When I know that Charlie is the better choice for her and yet, I want her to pick me.

THE REST of the week passes quickly but not without my carving out time to see Celine. Once I'm back from Dallas, I drop off a morning coffee before she's due on set. The following day, I decorate her front porch with hay bales and pumpkins and a small scarecrow Bea pointed out when we took Gran to the garden center to buy mums.

CELINE

Ahh!! I love this season!

CELINE

(Sends picture of front porch)

BEAU

I know. You're the weirdo who likes Halloween best.

CELINE

I know! Halloween is in four days! How did we not discuss this sooner?

CELINE

What are you dressing up as?

BEAU

A hockey player.

CELINE

Ha. Ha. Come on! Give me something to work with...

CELINE

(GIF of Tarzan and Jane)

CELINE

(Image of a regal, regency-themed couple)

BEAU

Bridgerton? No way.

CELINE

Cosmo and Wanda?

BEAU

No one will recognize the fairy godparents from The Fairy OddParents.

CELINE:

YOU JUST DID!

BEAU

I hate to do this, but I have a game that night.

CELINE

Seriously?

BEAU

Seriously.

CELINE

So, I have to pass out candy alone?

BEAU

Also hate to break it to you but…no one, and I literally mean no one, is going to trick-or-treat out at the Klingers' place.

CELINE

(Three crying emojis)

BEAU

Go to Gran's? Bea will be there, passing out candy, as Gran pretends to put a hex on all the children.

CELINE

(Two laughing emojis)

CELINE

I'll see if they'll take me.

BEAU

They will.

CELINE

I know. I'll bring Hocus Pocus.

BEAU

The original?

CELINE

I'm always impressed that you know these things. Yes, the original.

BEAU

Gotta go but expect a package on your doorstep tomorrow. It's from me—and therefore, safe.

CELINE

What'd you get me?

CELINE

Beau! I hate surprises.

CELINE

And you know that about me.

CELINE

(Three eyeroll emojis)

THE NEXT MORNING, I leave my hockey jersey and a ticket to Friday night's game on her doorstep.

Just as I turn to descend the porch steps, her front door swings open.

She stands, wedged between the door and the doorjamb, her hair piled messily on her head. She's wearing a silk pink robe that slips off one shoulder and her cheek still has a pillow line from sleep.

I grin. "Good morning, beautiful."

She smirks. "Are you woo-ing me?"

I snort.

"Because I'm not opposed to being wooed."

"I didn't think you were." I step back onto the porch, cross my arms over my chest, and lean back against a pillar.

"One week of being attentive doesn't mean I've forgotten the past."

My chest tightens at her words. "I know."

She holds the door open wider. "But I'm getting there." Then she turns and walks into her kitchen. My eyes zero in on her ass as I step over the threshold and close the door.

Celine's pink robe is a puddle on the floor, her gorgeous body naked, beckoning me forward as she disappears into her bedroom.

I step out of my shoes and pop the button on my jeans but don't lose them completely. I don't want to be presumptuous but... I *want* to be presumptuous.

"Celine?" I call out.

Her laughter fills the space.

"Cece, for real?"

She laughs harder this time.

I walk deeper into her place, loiter by the door to her bedroom.

Celine turns, gives me a playful look over her shoulder.

The breath is knocked out of my lungs as I take in her naked form, from behind. Fuck if she's not the hottest woman I've ever seen in my life. Smooth, tanned skin, sweet dimples flashing before the delectable curves of her ass. A nipped waist that flares into hips I want to sink my fingertips into.

"Celine." My voice holds a warning.

She spins on her heel and falls back onto her bed, the sheets still rumpled from sleep. Pushing up onto her elbows, she bends one knee, her glorious body on full display, tempting the hell out of me.

"Two can play this game, Turner."

I snort but the sound is muffled as I tug off my shirt. "What game, babe?"

"Wooing." She smirks. "Now come on, make my morning." Her voice drips with confidence that hits me like a shot of adrenaline. It's sexy, how sure of herself she is. How much she knows what she wants.

Right now, Celine Hernandez wants *me*. I move closer to the bed and drop over her, kissing her hard. Then, I give her everything she's asking for. Twice.

EIGHTEEN
CELINE

"AREN'T YOU CUTE?" Bea comments as I slip into the passenger side of the car she's driving.

I grin. "Nice ride."

She rolls her eyes. "It's Cole's."

"No kidding," I joke, glancing around. The inside of Cole's car is pristine; there's even one of those throwback tree air fresheners hanging from the rearview mirror. I tap it for emphasis and Bea sticks her tongue out at me.

It's no secret that Bea's car—most of Bea's space—is a mess, sprinkled with dusty clay from her pottery and cluttered in a way that fills most of her family with stress.

I lean back in my seat and pull on the seat belt as Bea eases out of the driveway. "I haven't been to a hockey game in years," I tell her.

She glances at me as she turns onto the road. "Since you and Beau dated long or…"

I scrunch up my nose. "I've been to two Kings games since I moved out to California," I reference LA's NHL team. "But both of those were more for networking or showing up as a favor to a friend, not to *watch* the game."

She smirks. "You remember all the lingo?"

I swat her, laughing. "I know that Beau's save percentage this season is currently 0.928."

Bea whistles. "You're back! Best puck bunny on the—"

I swat her again and she cracks up, flashing me a smile. "I miss you and Beau together, Celine. This, right now, it feels like old times."

"Yeah. Except you're driving instead of sitting in a booster seat," I deadpan. Even though Bea is only four and a half years younger than me, she's been like my little sister since I met her. But she's right. This does feel like old times.

A thrill rolls down my spine as the excitement of watching Beau play live again spikes. When we were together, I went to all his high school games. I drew his number on my cheek with black eyeliner, wore his jersey, and cheered him on through every win and loss of his high school career. I traveled to most of his away games in the state and never missed any of the big games.

My parents hated it, worried my time spent following Beau around would distract me from my grades or college applications. They were horrified that I planned to pursue a career in acting and forgo college altogether. Eventually, they came around, especially once I found success on *Midnight Moon*. But during the years when I didn't have their support, I leaned on Beau. I found refuge at Gran's. I had the Turner family.

Singing along to old tunes, riding to Beau's game, with Bea feels right. It's an energy shift, sliding me back into a place I used to call home. Again, it hits me how long it's been since I've felt this way. Is it nostalgia? Or is it more?

Is this—right here, right now—the life I should be embracing instead of the glitzy, Hollywood one I've stepped into?

When Bea pulls into the arena and parks, I take a moment to study The Honeycomb. For years, Beau dreamed of playing hockey at the NHL level. When he enlisted—wanting to do right by his siblings and Gran—I never thought I'd see him in an NHL jersey. And yet, here he is.

I breathe in, looking up at the arena with wonder. Beau Turner and I chased our dreams so hard and look where we made it—he's a goalie for the Thunderbolts and I'm one of the highest paid female actresses in Hollywood.

But I can't help wondering about the sacrifices we made. Namely, each other.

"You ready?" Bea prompts.

"Yep." I fall into step beside her as we enter the arena.

Due to the passes Beau secured us, we bypass a lot of the lines and are whisked through a series of hallways by two burly security guards. One of them, John, Caleb arranged for me since I gave him the weekend off to attend his nephew's birthday party. The other guy works at the arena and he and Bea fall into easy conversation. He leaves us in front of a cupcake stand and Bea chuckles.

"This is where I used to work." She waves a hand in front of Primrose Sweets. The line is crazy long and from the comments I overhear, the cupcakes are solid.

"I can't believe this is where you started out and now, you're weeks away from opening your shop!" I squeeze her hard as we stand at the end of the line.

"I know," Bea breathes out. Her eyes are wide, her hair a perfect tumble of curls. "I can't believe it either. I'm such a ball of nervous energy and giddy butterflies about the whole thing."

"It's going to be great. I can't wait for the opening."

"Bree, Meg, and I have been working around the clock."

"It will be worth it," I reassure her.

"Bea! I thought that was you," a female voice says.

Bea and I turn. Bea smiles and pulls the woman into a hug. "Noelle! I didn't know you'd be here tonight."

"It was last minute." Noelle pulls back slightly, still holding onto Bea's upper arms. "I had a meeting cancellation and decided to join Scott. You guys are going to give us a run for our money tonight." She glances at the long line. "Come on, I have a whole bunch of cupcakes and coffees in the box. Let's catch up for a few."

Bea gives me a searching look and I shrug, falling into step with them.

"Noelle, this is Beau's girlfriend—"

"Celine Hernandez," Noelle cuts Bea off, grinning. "I didn't want to be an awkward fan but, too late." She beams and I laugh. "I freaking love *Midnight Moon*!"

"Oh, thank you," I say, shaking her hand.

"Noelle started Primrose Sweets in Boston, where she met her husband, Scott Reland. He owns the Boston Hawks."

I gasp. "The competition."

Noelle's eyebrows dance. "Exactly!"

The three of us laugh as Noelle gestures us into a private box. John remains at the entrance, standing guard as I slip inside. We sit around a high-top table as Noelle sets out some cupcakes and coffees. A few curious gazes turn in our direction but everyone in this suite is either too polite or too used to the celebrity world to interrupt our chat.

I listen as Bea and Noelle fall into a comfortable conversation. After a few minutes of small talk, Noelle asks Bea questions about her business, listening thoughtfully and offering advice. I realize that Bea has found a mentor in Noelle and my pride for my surrogate little sister swells.

I love that Bea has stepped out of the large shadows of her successful big brothers, developed her own niche, and sought the advice of a fierce but friendly businesswoman to support her development.

As they chat, I glance out over the ice. The arena is packed, with fans wearing mostly Bolts orange but some clusters of Hawks blue. Group cheers and songs ring out. Entertainment in the form of a phenomenal figure skating duo takes the ice for a fundraising event. Popcorn flies, pretzels dripping in butter are munched on, and beer sloshes over the rims of plastic cups.

I settle back in my seat and watch with rapt attention. From my seat, no one can really see me, and I have the opportunity to drink in Beau's world without camera lenses and flashing lights.

I revel in it. I love being wrapped up in his dream.

The teams are announced, and I watch as my man—the one I've loved for most of my life—takes the ice. I clap and let out a whistle but realize when Beau's eyes swing to the stands, that he doesn't know I'm here. I'm sitting in the wrong box!

I turn to Bea, and I must look slightly panicked because she gives an amused laugh. Noelle's look is knowing. They hug good-bye.

"Come on, let's relocate," Bea says.

I smile sheepishly at Noelle. "It's wonderful to meet you."

"Trust me, it's better meeting you," she volleys.

I laugh.

"Forgive us for being so wrapped up in Bea's new store. I lost track of time and—"

"It's okay," I reassure Noelle. "It's been a long time since I've been in a hockey arena. It's nice for me to sit back and take it all in."

"Hope our paths cross again," Noelle offers as she walks us to the door. She pats a man's shoulder as we pass. He's deep in conversation but brushes a finger over the nape of her neck. When his green eyes pass over me, recognition flairs in their depths. Noelle laughs. "My husband will be gutted to miss meeting you. *Midnight Moon* is our show."

"Next time," Bea says, linking our arms together. "I have a feeling Celine may stick around."

Noelle smiles. "I hope so. Enjoy the game, ladies."

"See you, Noelle," Bea says as I thank her.

Once we're out of the private box, Bea and I glance at each

other. An unspoken understanding passes between us, and we take off at a run. John scrambles after us, calling out for us to slow down. But we're breathless with laughter, sprinting to the box filled with wives and girlfriends, knowing that our men are looking for us.

We don't want to let them down.

"HEY!" Bea greets a group of women who make room for us in the Bolts' WAGs box.

"You're here!" A beautiful blonde with sparkling blue eyes stands and pulls Bea into a hug.

Bea hugs her back. "Maisy, this is Celine." She introduces me before pointing to the other women. "Mila, Harper, and" —she pauses before indicating a woman bouncing a sweet infant on her hip—"Indy Scotch, the coach's wife and the other coach's daughter."

Indy blushes. "Thanks for coming tonight."

I smile and give a little wave. "Nice to meet y'all. I'm—"

"Celine Hernandez," they say in unison before blushing wildly and giggling.

I like them all immediately and plop down into a vacant seat. "Celine," I confirm.

"And you're here for Beau!" The woman named Maisy screeches, clasping her hands in genuine excitement.

"Way to play it cool." Mila elbows her.

Harper snorts and smiles at me warmly. "It's good to see Beau so happy."

"Yeah," Mila agrees.

"He's definitely beating up Axel less," Maisy comments.

Bea grins. "As if anyone could beat up Axel."

Harper leans closer to me. "His nickname is Brawler."

"He lives up to it on the ice," Bea explains. "Not so much in real life."

I shake my head a little, indicating my confusion.

"Axel has a twenty-one-year-old daughter," Maisy says.

"Lola," Mila cuts in, before dropping her voice. "We're all pretty sure—"

"We're taking bets," Harper interjects.

"That River Patton, the right wing, is sweet on her." Mila points to a player.

I pick up the coffee cup I took to-go from Noelle's box and take a sip. "There's a lot to unpack here."

Maisy laughs. "You have no idea."

The women continue to chat and laugh, pulling me into their fold easily. I keep one ear tuned into their conversation —Mila begging Maisy to pick a wedding date now that she and Axel are engaged, speculation about a guy named Cohen's dating life, Harper's shopping experience with Damien's mother—but my eyes are glued to the ice.

I watch the game with fascination. I love seeing Beau live out his childhood dream. I love being here to support and cheer for him. And when his eyes flash to the box and find me sitting here, among his teammates' girlfriends, I love the pride that washes through them.

It's something I've known deep down for years and desperately want to feel secure enough to embrace again. I am in love with Beau Turner.

Distance, heartache, and time hasn't changed a thing when it comes to me and him.

NINETEEN
BEAU

A BUZZER BEATER SAVE.

The team goes fucking wild, rushing me, smacking my helmet, screaming in my ear. An up-and-coming team like the Bolts isn't supposed to win against a powerhouse like the Hawks. But we did it, winning 3-2.

Adrenaline, excitement, even a little pride, swims through my veins. It's an emotional cocktail with a kick and I welcome it. After months of feeling on edge, riddled with anxiety and worry, with exhaustion and doubt, it feels incredible to have done something right.

Tonight, I didn't let my team down. Tonight, I lived the life I swore I would. Knowing that Celine witnessed it is the cherry on top, elevating this great moment into an incredible one.

I laugh with my teammates, gratefully accepting their shoulder smacks. Coach Scotch pulls me aside with a "good game, Turner," comment that feels like another win. Weeks of sparring with Brawler has cleared my head but knowing that my improvement is noticed by Coach takes it to the next level.

I'm riding a natural high and I feel fucking invincible.

The way I used to in high school, with a big C on my chest for captain, and my beautiful girl tucked under my arm.

The energy in the locker room crackles like electricity. The team was on tonight, everyone gelled. Even River, who's always scowling, cracks a smile.

"Drinks!" Damien hollers. "I want to see everyone's ugly face at Corks tonight."

"Hey!" Devon shoves him good-naturedly. "This face could be on a damn billboard in Times Square." He gives a serious model look.

Damien snickers. "You're just sore because I was voted the Hottest Bolt on the Hottest Hockey Heroes blog."

Axel rolls his eyes, muttering under his breath.

Devon scowls. River smirks. Cole chuckles.

I let out a deep breath, loving the ease of this moment. A huge weight lifted from my shoulders tonight and for once, I want to celebrate with the team. I'm not going to Corks to "show my face" so the team doesn't talk and wonder what's up with me. I'm not going out with friends to appease Gran and Bea. I'm going because I want to.

It's another step in the right direction.

I shower quickly, dress in dark jeans and a black Henley, and grab my truck keys and wallet. Stepping into the hallway after the game, I clock Celine immediately. She's standing with my sister and the other Bolts girls. They're chatting easily. From Celine's body language, I know she's comfortable with Maisy and the girls. I pause, just taking her in.

I love that she's here tonight. The fact that she's wearing my jersey, the way she used to, makes some of the cracks in my chest heal. Seeing her hang with my friends' girls eases some of the worries I've had.

I've missed Celine Hernandez in every way imaginable for nearly a decade. This moment, right now, almost makes all that missing worth it. Because I cherish her being here more than I did in high school. Now, it's not a given. Now, it's a choice and I need to know that on some level, she'll choose me. Us. This.

She shifts and when her eyes catch mine, the most breath-taking smile crosses her lips. "Beau!"

The girls clap and cheer as I approach.

"Nice save," Mila tosses out.

"Good game, Beau," Maisy says, patting my back.

I nod at their words, but my eyes are trained on Celine. She tosses her arms around my shoulders, and I pull her close as lightbulbs flash around us.

"You were incredible, Beau," she murmurs before kissing me hard.

More cameras angle in our direction.

"Our secret's out, babe," she giggles as another round of flashes go off.

Celine is unconcerned but something in my stomach sours.

Why does this moment—one I've been yearning for, one I want to hold on to—need to be tainted for others' eyes? I know the media is waiting for comments about the game, but I also know that with Celine here, they're going to ask about our history, if we're dating, and the news tomorrow will be more about Celine and Beau than the Thunderbolts incredible win against the Hawks.

Once I confirm that Cole has Bea, Celine and I move down the hall toward the exit.

"Great save, Turner!" one of the regular reporters calls out. "Are you and Celine dating?"

"Beau, is this a second chance at love?" another one asks.

"Hey Celine, how's it feel being back home?" a third one chimes in.

"Celine, does this mean you and Charlie have called it quits?"

"Are you and Beau dating?"

"How long have you been seeing each other?"

"Are you making it official?"

Celine gives general smiles and dips her head, tucking her frame into mine as I do my best to shield her from the hurling questions and flashing cameras. My agitation rises quickly, replacing my good vibes with sour ones.

"Why can't they leave you alone?" I mutter to my girl.

She shrugs. "This is part of my life now." Her words are easy, but I hear the current of worry in her tone.

As much as I want to reassure her that it doesn't bother me—the way everyone in the country seems to have a piece of her, the way paparazzi and reporters hound her for information—I can't. Because I'd be lying. I'm infinitely proud of Celine and her success but I don't like to be front and center. I prefer to live behind the scenes, where noises and lights don't bring flashbacks, where my actions aren't constantly scrutinized by others.

I manage to shake off the questioning by flipping a general comment about how great the team played tonight. As we reach the doors, Celine's security guard, who gave her space tonight but never left, steps forward. He escorts us to my truck, holding off the swarms of fans calling out both our names.

Once we're in my truck, Celine gives me a shaky smile. "Sorry about that."

"Don't be." My voice is tighter than it was in the locker room. I heave out a sigh, wanting to shake off the damper that the media and their incessant questions plunged me in.

Celine's hand rests on my thigh and her touch centers me. I place my hand on hers and squeeze. "You were amazing, Beau."

I smile at her. "I'm glad you were here tonight, Cece. Thanks for coming."

"It was my pleasure. Your friends, the girls…it's a great group."

"Yeah. You want to head to Corks for drinks?"

She nods, smiling. "Let me text John so he can beef up security if needed." She moves her hand to send her security guard a text.

I sigh, hating that she needs to take these extra safety measures but also grateful that she is. I don't say anything as I pull out of The Honeycomb. As the arena falls into my rearview, my annoyance melts away and I'm able to enjoy the moment with Celine once more.

When we pull up to Corks, it's mayhem.

"Just pull up front," she advises. "Mitch came and he'll take care of your truck. John already spoke with the owner and they're controlling the number of people inside."

I do as Celine says. As I step out of my truck, I'm practically pushed back by the number of people who surge forward, most with camera phones, to get a photo of Celine. I work a swallow, my number one priority my girl, and round the truck to open her door.

John beats me to it and as he escorts her into Corks, I watch as she maneuvers through the bodies and voices, giving a little wave and flashing a smile, before dipping inside.

How does she manage it so effortlessly?

The crowd sets me on edge. The voices calling her name shred my nerves. The fact that everyone wants her attention fills me with worry.

"Good game, Turner," the owner, Bill, calls out as I enter the bar. "We're restricting capacity tonight."

I pause to shake his hand. "Thanks, Bill." I look outside at the growing crowd. Tension pulls through my shoulders. The back of my neck prickles. My skin feels too tight. "You sure? This could be a big night and—"

"I'm sure," he cuts me off, glancing at his bar. "This space provides the Coyotes and the Bolts with a place to blow off steam. No way am I compromising that for one crazy night."

I dip my head in understanding and thanks.

"We're letting a lot of the regulars in. Some of the Coyotes players are here." He points to the bar where I spot Cohen and Leo from the football team. "You take it easy and have a pint. You earned it."

I chuckle, looking to where Celine waits for me, halfway between the door and the bar. "Thanks again, Bill."

He nods before moving back toward the door to man the entrance.

I tuck Celine under my arm, and we make our way toward the bar.

"This is bananas," Maisy comments as we reach the bar.

I note that Bill has some of the blinds down, restricting eyes to this side of the bar to give us some privacy.

"Girl, I don't know how you do it," Mila comments, voicing my concerns aloud. "I can't imagine having this kind of reaction every time I step outside my house."

Celine shrugs. "It's not that bad. In LA, where I live, no one blinks twice. And since I've been here, tucked away in the country, I've found a slice of solitude. I think it's more the speculation that Beau and I are back together."

"Everyone loves a second chance romance," Harper agrees, slipping onto a barstool.

"Hey." Damien steps beside me, gripping my shoulder. Then, he holds out a hand to Celine. "I'm Damien."

"Nice to meet you. Celine." She shakes his hand before introducing herself to Leo and Cohen.

"They're the enemy," Damien explains, good-naturedly pointing to the football players.

Leo chuckles. "What're you drinking, Celine? Beau, your first beer's on me. That was one hell of a save."

"Thanks, man," I say as Leo calls over the bartender, Saffron.

Some of the staff move tables to create a bit of a private area for the Bolts as we take up more space at the bar. My teammates introduce themselves to Celine and carefully erect a wall to keep her in the center, where it's harder for patrons to snap her photo.

My gratitude for my team multiplies tenfold as I watch them silently step up to make sure Celine is protected, to squash some of my nerves that everyone knows I battle but no one publicly comments on.

"To Beau's save." Devon holds his pint high and shoots me a wink. His eyes slide to Celine, and I scoff at his double meaning—saving the game, saving my chance with this girl.

"Cheers!" Damien hollers.

We all drink to the night, to this moment. I savor the refreshing taste of my beer and the feel of Celine's body as her curves sink into my frame. I wrap an arm around her, my hand resting on her hip.

"Where's River?" Axel asks.

"He's coming," Cole replies, but I note the dip of concern in between his eyebrows.

Harper shoots Celine a knowing glance and when Celine snorts, I wonder what the hell is going on. Even though I don't know, I like that my girl is in on it. I like that she fits into my life.

"Hey, Celine, you free the weekend after next?" Damien asks.

I raise an eyebrow at my teammate.

"Oh! That's right," Maisy cuts in. "You have to come to Friendsgiving."

"We're hosting," Harper explains, grinning at Damien.

"Friendsgiving?" I ask.

Mila gives me a sympathetic look. "You're ignoring the group text again, aren't you?"

I scoff. "Y'all message every five seconds."

"Beau's fucking right," Devon agrees.

Mila grins. "Friendsgiving is weekend after next. Y'all are playing Halloween *and* Thanksgiving weekend this year."

Celine tips her head back to look up at me.

"You wanna go?" I murmur so only she can hear.

She studies me for a long moment. An almost-shy look crosses her face before she nods. At her confirmation, my residual aggravation fades away and I smile. I kiss the tip of her nose.

"Aww," Maisy murmurs, clutching her heart.

"Obvious!" Mila elbows her.

"We're in," I announce.

"You gonna extend an invite to us?" Leo asks, gesturing between him and Cohen.

The Bolts guys all chuckle but it turns to a groan when Maisy nods enthusiastically and Harper says, "Of course you're invited!"

As the drinks flow, country music plays over the speakers. Celine and I are wrapped up in the conversation of my team and I relax fully. Keeping my girl tucked under my arm, I enjoy the moment.

Her. Us. This.

TWENTY
CELINE

"HAPPY TO SEE ME?" Charlie asks, dropping his shoulder bag on a chair inside my trailer.

My eyes dart to his and I smile, standing from my chair to hug him hello.

"Celine!" my makeup artist scolds me.

I squeeze Charlie once before dropping back into the chair. "Sorry," I tell Maribel. "You're early," I say to Charlie.

He snorts.

I smile. "But I'm happy you're here."

"Yeah?" As soon as he asks the question, my stomach tightens. By the way he shoves his hands in his pockets and dips his chin, I know he's hoping for more than what I'm capable of giving.

I couldn't give Charlie the commitment he sought years ago because I was hung up on Beau. Now, I'm over the moon about Beau and realize everything I felt for Charlie can only be described as friendship with an extra level of understanding and companionship when we both were feeling low.

I open my mouth to gently tell him we need to talk when a knock sounds on my trailer. My PA, Mellie, pokes her head in. "You needed to be on set about"—she pauses to glance at her

Apple Watch—"two minutes and twenty seconds ago. Also, Beau's here."

At the mention of Beau, Charlie rears back slightly. I read the surprise, followed by a flare of disappointment, in his eyes. Then, his jaw clenches and he drops his head. Is it in understanding? Resignation? A challenge?

I have no idea because Mellie whisks me toward the door of the trailer with Maribel following in our wake.

"Let me just spray this." Maribel waves her setting spray.

I pause. "Sorry—argh!" I cough as a cloud of setting spray fills my mouth.

"Sorry," Maribel whispers, turning away.

"I gotta go," I tell Charlie.

"It's okay. Go. I'll catch up with you," he mutters as I exit.

"What a shitshow," Mellie murmurs as she grips my arm and pulls me along.

"Tell me about it," I reply.

"He looks good though."

"Charlie?"

She snorts. "Him too."

I laugh.

Mellie's eyes glitter. "Wait till you see Beau."

We turn a corner. The set opens before us. But my eyes snag on Beau and hold because, "Damn," I murmur.

"Right?" Mellie agrees.

Beau Turner has always been the type of guy that turns heads. But right now, in a form-fitting white button-down, rolled up on his forearms, and a casual pair of ripped jeans, leaning against a table talking to one of the camera guys, he looks phenomenal. His hair is styled, he's in a pair of Jordans, and he looks a hell of a lot less like the guy who drives around with a toolbox in the bed of his truck and more like the man who will whisk me off set to wine and dine me before taking me to the penthouse at the Premier Hotel.

I like both versions immensely. But since I think Beau

upped his game because of Charlie's arrival, a ripple of excitement runs through me. Beau stepping up his wardrobe means he views Charlie as competition. He has nothing to worry about, especially with my feelings as they are. But…a little jealousy isn't a bad thing when I've been hoping for this man's favor for nearly a decade.

"Celine!" the director calls my name.

Mellie and I both snap to attention. We share a glance and a giggle before I switch into actor mode and stride onto set, ready to work.

Thad gives me a quick wink before shooting begins. As soon as "action" is called, everything that is happening around me fades. I give my mind and body over to the scene, tuning out distractions and pouring all of myself into my character. Her feelings, her emotions, her motivations and desires. Nothing else matters.

Thad and I film two scenes, doing several takes until the director is satisfied. I'm not sure if minutes or hours pass because time stands still when I'm acting. I know it's a dream to turn one's passion into their career and it's something I never take for granted.

"Cut!"

The director's voice pulls me from the moment.

"Nice work, Hernandez," Thad says in a low voice.

I grin at him. "You too. Quite the doting man," I say, referencing his character's devotion and commitment to my character's healing process after she leaves an abusive relationship.

"Could say that about them too." Thad tips his head off set.

I turn. "Shit," I mutter.

Thad chuckles.

Beau and Charlie are standing beside each other. Their arms are crossed over their chests, their biceps popping. Although they're engaged in conversation, they're both facing forward, neither giving the other an inch. It's clear that they're posturing. Both seeking the upper hand in whatever they're discussing.

As if realizing that filming has stopped, both men's eyes snap to mine.

Thad's laughter grows. "Go get 'em, girl."

I walk toward the guys and watch as their presences seem to expand. It's ridiculous really, but I know that my actions right now will speak louder than any words I say.

If I move toward Charlie, I'll be sending Beau a signal. If I move toward Beau, I'll be giving Charlie a heads-up that we need to talk.

I step into Beau's side, relax as his hand finds the small of my back and rests there.

He smiles at me, the slate in his eyes warming to cobalt.

I clear my throat, ignore the hurt that washes over Charlie's expression, and say, "Beau, this is one of my closest friends in the industry, Charlie. Charlie, meet Beau."

"We've already exchanged pleasantries, Cel," Charlie says.

Beau dips his head in agreement.

I force a smile. "Great. Is anyone hungry for lunch?"

Both men make agreeable sounds, although I know neither of them really wants to have lunch with the other. However, they're sucking it up and doing it for me. The realization soothes me, but I don't want to endure an awkward lunch.

To save the situation, I call Thad over.

When my costar turns in my direction, I give him a mischievous smirk. "You hungry?"

He laughs, his gaze flashing between Charlie and Beau. "You're used to getting your way, aren't you?"

I shrug.

He walks over and joins our circle, greeting Beau and Charlie. Winking at me, he mutters, "The sweetheart and all her admirers."

Beau snorts, Charlie scowls, and I laugh.

Then, we relocate to my trailer where Mellie has called in a delicious spread. I force her to join us too and...lunch is served.

"YOU HANDLED THAT WELL," Thad assures me as we walk back onto set for filming.

While lunch had threads of tension, most of the awkwardness dissipated as soon as Charlie realized that Beau and I are serious about each other. That, coupled with Beau's willingness to get to know Charlie, and Charlie's good-naturedness, smoothed over any issues.

By the end of the meal, Charlie and Beau were discussing DC comics like they've been friends since grade school.

"You were a good buffer," I reply.

He chuckles easily. "You up for returning the favor?"

I look at him in surprise.

His smile is cryptic.

"The cowboy?" I guess.

He shakes his head. "The *one*."

Excitement for my colleague-turned-friend flows. "Seriously?"

He shrugs. "It's too early to tell but, if it happens—"

"I'll be whatever buffer you need," I promise.

Thad slugs an arm over my shoulder. "You're a good egg, Hernandez."

"Yeah. And I don't crack," I assure him.

He laughs. "I can tell."

"We're ready when you are," the director says.

Thad and I resume our places on set and once again, I give myself over to my character. But this time, I feel more settled.

It's an inner energy shift that I can't explain but I feel it. My mind is clearer, my thoughts less questioning.

I slip into character and believe that this performance is my best to date.

Because never in my life have I felt so at peace with my choices. With the future I want to create.

After two hours of filming, the director calls it a day. I head back to my trailer, knowing that Beau took off a while ago to attend a team meeting.

I left Charlie keys to my house, and I wonder if he headed there to take a nap. I'm planning to stay at Beau's while Charlie's in town, but I need to swing home to grab some clothes. I enter the trailer.

"Hey." Charlie looks up from the book he's reading.

"Hi." I plop down into another chair and reach for a packet of makeup remover wipes. "I figured you'd be sleeping."

"Nah. Slept on the flight. You were great today," he says. "It was really good to see you in action."

His words assuage some of the guilt I feel that I know this visit isn't going to pan out the way he hoped. "Thanks. I'm glad you came."

"Me too."

"For tomorrow night, there's a dinner—"

"I'm not going to stay," Charlie cuts me off, shifting forward in his chair.

"Because of Beau?" I guess.

"I like him," Charlie admits. "And I can tell you're happy with him."

"I really am."

"But I came here to see if there could be anything more between us. I've been waiting a long time, Celine. Timing for us never really lined up and I know now that it never will."

"I'm sorry," I whisper.

"Don't be." He shakes his head. "More than anything, I

want to see you happy. And if Beau is the man who does that for you, then you should be with him. I wouldn't want either of us to settle for less."

"Me neither. And I never meant to give you false hope or mixed signals."

"You didn't. You were always honest and upfront about your past with Beau. When you started filming here, I wondered if you would get back together with him. I wondered if you wanted this role to see if you could get back together with him." He sighs, "I worried I'd lose you."

"We'll always be friends, Charlie." I lean forward to grab his hand. "We've been through a lot together. Our lives changed overnight, together."

"We'll always be friends," he confirms, giving me a squeeze back. "But I realize now I never truly had you, Celine. Not the way Beau holds a piece of your heart. And it's okay. Honestly, it's better this way because now I can move on too and stop holding on to hope that things between us will develop into more."

His words are spoken simply, injected with honesty that I appreciate even though I hate that I've hurt him. "You're a good man, Charlie. And a good friend."

"Yeah," he murmurs, dropping my hand and sitting back in his seat. "If you don't mind, I'll crash at your place tonight."

"Of course."

"And be on my way in the morning."

"I don't have to be on set until noon. Brunch?" I offer, smiling at him.

He chuckles. "Yeah, Celine. We'll do brunch. See if Beau wants to join."

I beam at him, and he shakes his head. "Can't believe I've been upstaged by a hockey player," he mutters, playfully.

I wrinkle my nose. "It's always been the hockey player."

Charlie groans and clutches his chest. "Don't kick a man when he's down."

"You won't be down for long, Charlie. You'll find the right woman and when you do, Beau and I will fly out to meet her."

"Holding you to that, Hernandez."

I dip my head in agreement. Again, an internal shift takes place. Lightness replaces some of the worry I've carried around. My life in Tennessee offers a serenity, an inclusion, a *knowing*, that I never truly felt in LA.

Here, I feel at home.

TWENTY-ONE
BEAU

AFTER CHARLIE'S VISIT, Celine and I settle into a new normal. She spends more nights at my place. When she has a late shooting, I wait up for her to arrive home. We squeeze in meals together, whether on set or at The Honeycomb or Gran's house.

We're us again and it feels more natural than breathing. We're both juggling hectic schedules and multiple commitments, but we're making time for each other.

The only cloud hovering in my newly discovered blue sky is the media. The paparazzi have been out in full force since Charlie's appearance. While he's now holidaying with a former costar in Mexico, even his beach vacation hasn't pulled attention off Celine.

Instead, she's constantly hounded with questions. Did she break Charlie's heart? Have they called it quits for good? Are she and I planning a wedding? Will she relocate to Tennessee? Are any of the rumors about her and Thad true? Did Charlie and I get into an altercation? Is that why his trip was cut short?

In truth, it's exhausting. But Celine handles it with a quiet grace and level head. I, on the other hand, feel like I'm bursting at the seams. I hate having people in my private space. Camping outside my condo building. Loitering on the lawn outside Gran's house. Filling the halls of The Honeycomb.

The paparazzi presence, coupled with their incessant questions and flashbulbs, has me on edge. I'm walking a thin line and as the pressure, mixed with anxiety and fear, mounts each day, I know it's only a matter of time before I snap.

Every time I bring it up to Celine, she says we'll navigate it together. I know she's trying to understand my concerns. She's set boundaries with certain paparazzi and agreed to answer questions if they'll give me more space. As much as I appreciate her efforts, the constant hounding unnerves me.

Blowing off steam in the gym has become my new go-to. I rerack the bar before sitting up and reaching for my water bottle.

"You wanna spar?" Axel asks, reading my shitty mood.

"Nah," I answer honestly. As much as Axel and boxing have helped clear my mind, they also indicated a deeper issue.

One I am planning to rectify by taking Cole up on his offer to find me a therapist.

Devon glances at me. "You good?"

I sigh and take another pull of water. "This paparazzi shit is getting old."

"Man, they were swarming Corks the other night," River agrees. When River Patton gets where you're coming from, you know you have a fucking problem.

"They're everywhere. In the parking lot, outside my place, near Celine's and Gran's houses." I run a towel over my face to check some of my anger. "Always running their mouths and taking fucking photos."

"You talk to Celine about it?" Axel asks.

I nod. "She's trying to negotiate with them. Give them time to snap photos or answer questions if they'll back off.

But I hate that she needs to do that for me. She also beefed up security near her place."

Damien sighs. "If it's becoming an issue for you…" He trails off.

I shrug. "I gotta get it under control, right?"

The guys are silent.

"That why you're putting in extra time in here?" Damien correctly guesses.

"Yep," I say, popping the "p."

The guys are quiet again. This time, longer than before.

"Everyone has their breaking point," Devon finally mutters.

I force a smile to let him know I've got it under control. That I'm not going to snap or break or fall apart.

But it's bullshit. Because when I leave The Honeycomb and move toward my truck, a paparazzo jumps out at me from behind a parked car. The sudden movement, his rapid-fire question, has me coiling into a defensive position.

His eyes widen and he shuffles back two steps. "Hey, take it easy, man," he mutters, as if I'm the one invading his personal space.

I hold up a hand in warning and stalk past him without responding. But even after I start my truck and pull out of the parking lot, my fingers shake and my breathing is erratic.

The guy scared the shit out of me. More than that, his presence angered me on a level I know isn't normal. I want to lash out. I want to snap or break or unravel.

And it's getting harder to pretend otherwise.

"LOOK AT THIS PLACE." Bodhi holds his hands out to the side.

I glance at my brother, smile when I note how hard he's

cheesing. We're standing outside of Humble Bee's, Bea's newest venture with two of her friends and fellow potters.

"It looks incredible," I agree, taking in the storefront.

A rustic, oak bench sits outside, adorned with various greenery and flowers in pots that showcase Bea's signature style. The big window is lit up and the store is filled with customers, friends, and family, all gathering to celebrate Bea, Bree, and Meg on their launch.

"I'm proud of her," Celine says.

I slip my arm around her waist and pull her close. "Me too."

Since my parents passed, I shouldered the responsibility of being more than just a brother to my siblings. With Bea, the youngest and the only female, the responsibility multiplied. Would my brothers and I be enough for her? Were we guiding her down the right path? Would she be okay?

Standing here now, staring at the store she started, I know my parents would be proud of her. Of all of us for sticking together and making bigger lives than anyone imagined in the wake of their deaths.

A movement from the corner of my eye pulls my attention and I straighten when I spot a paparazzo standing a few feet away. My grip on Celine tightens.

"Don't they ever back off?" I mutter.

Following my gaze, Celine sighs. "I'll go talk to him."

"No." I hold her closer. I hate that she feels the need to protect me when it should be the other way around.

I glance at Caleb and he nods, letting me know that they'll tighten security as needed. What a way to live.

Bodhi ushers us into the shop and I know it's partly because he knows I want to say something. React. Defend the woman I love.

"Baby Bea!" Bodhi calls out as soon as we cross the threshold and come face-to-face with our beautiful, talented, and overwhelmed sister.

"You're here! Thank God!" She grips Bodhi's biceps and pulls him in for a hug. "What do you think? Is it going okay? Do people look excited or bored? Disappointed? Oh gosh, do you think I misunderstood customer expectations?" Bea's words come out in a rush, and I know she's been considering the answers to these questions on an endless thought loop.

My frustration over the paparazzo outside subsides and my heart softens as I focus on my sister. Tonight is a big moment for her and I won't let someone else's bullshit distract me from celebrating Bea's success.

"It's perfect," Bodhi assures her.

She wrings her hands and I reach out to pull her into a hug. I kiss her temple. "You did good, kid."

She gives me a small smile as she pulls back. "Thank you. Thanks for coming."

Her attention turns toward Celine who pulls her into a warm embrace. "Are you kidding?" Celine laughs. "No way in hell I'd miss this."

"That's what I said," a big man guffaws.

Bea smiles at him. "Celine, Beau, Bodhi, meet Uncle Kirk."

I extend my hand to the man who raised Cole. "Good to meet you, sir."

"You too, Beau." He shakes my hand. "Thank you for your service."

At the genuine gratitude in his tone, my throat closes with emotion. It happens from time to time, when someone catches me in a particularly emotional moment. Or extends gratitude selflessly. Or seems to understand the burdens I carry on a deeper level.

Uncle Kirk hit all three criteria and I dip my head in thanks, while trying to clear the swell of emotion that moves through me.

"Come on, let me show you something." Bea pulls Celine and me away from the huddle as Bodhi engages Uncle Kirk in conversation.

I wave to Cole's cousin Jamie as she joins her dad and follow my sister to the back of the store. We have to move through throngs of people. I'm swept up in their energy, loving the commentary on the pottery pieces. I exchange quick hugs and congrats with Bree and Meg.

Bea twirls as we reach the back corner of the store. "For you." She places a box in my hand before passing one to Celine.

I smile at my sister, confused and also touched that she created something for Celine and me.

"Open them," she encourages. I note the flair of nerves mixed with a dash of excitement in her expression.

Celine opens her box and pulls out a shimmery gold mug that reads *Hollywood* in bold, black strokes. "Ooh, Bea! I love it!"

Bea grins. "I'm glad." She tips her head toward me, waiting for me to pull out my mug. "It's a twist on my new signature product, his and her mugs."

I open mine. It's a deep navy, covered in tiny, delicate white stars. *Star* is written in a gold script. I smirk, touched by Bea's thoughtfulness and the creative way she merged Celine's and my lives—the actress and the soldier—together. "This is awesome, Bea. Very thoughtful. Thank you."

Bea smiles, her grey eyes shiny with emotion. "I'm glad you like it."

"You think he's more of a star than me?" Celine asks, half joking to lighten the moment.

Bea's smile widens. "I love you, Cece. But this guy"—she links her arm with mine—"is my North Star. I wouldn't have made it here without you, Beau."

Jesus. Emotion clogs my throat so I can barely breathe. I pull my sister into my side and unlink our arms so I can wrap one around her. Hold her close. Tell her, without the words since I can't find them, how damn proud of her I am. "You did this, kid." I manage after a moment.

She shakes her head, gives me a watery smile. Glances around the space. "Nah. It was mostly you, Beau. I wouldn't have gone to art school without your support."

"I love you, Bea," I tell her, kissing the top of her head.

She squeezes me for an extra moment. "Love you more." She glances at Celine. "And you, too."

Celine chuckles but I know the emotional moment affected her.

"Go," Celine urges Bea toward the crowd. "Your fans are waiting."

My sister laughs. "That's something, coming from you."

Celine shakes her head. "Enjoy this moment, Bea. You earned it."

My sister blushes but ducks back into the crowd, instantly swept into conversation.

Celine looks at me. "You okay?"

I let out a shaky breath. "Yeah. She caught me off guard."

"She's one of the most pure-hearted women I know. You raised her right, Beau."

I nod again, the weight of the moment, the pride that Bea fills me with, pressing down on me. "I'm going to get some air."

"Okay," Celine falls into step beside me. "I'll keep you company." She links our arms as we make our way out through the back entrance. I need the cool, night air to shake off the emotions I'm drowning in.

We step outside and I breathe a sigh of relief.

Celine presses against me and her presence centers me. I love that she's here, sharing this moment with me and my family. I love that she loves my sister with the same intensity I do. I open my mouth to tell her how grateful I am that she's with me, back in my life, when a man bumps into me.

A camera thrusts into my face.

"Are you guys official now?" the man asks.

Celine stumbles back, caught off guard by his approach. I

grip her elbow to keep her from falling. In my periphery, Caleb rushes forward.

"Come on, Celine. Give me something to work with," the man carries on.

The anger that washes over me can only be described as blackout.

It's heavy and powerful, emanating from every pore I possess. One minute, the man is standing before me.

The next, he's on the ground, next to his shattered camera.

Celine's eyes are wide, her mouth open, as Caleb shields her.

Cell phones are out, recording the exchange.

My entire being is vibrating with fury as a string of expletives falls from my mouth. My hands are out, holding an invisible enemy at bay while I try to protect my woman who currently looks half scared of *me*.

Fuck. Realization dawns.

I snapped. I unraveled.

And now, Celine is looking at me like the monster I am.

The one I just brought out into the light.

The one that is currently being recorded on countless cell phones.

"Beau!" my sister gasps from the back door to her store.

Angry, humiliated, and desperate, I point at the injured paparazzo with the split lip. "Get the fuck away from my family."

TWENTY-TWO
CELINE

SHOCK SHOOTS through me like a live wire.

I take in the bloodied face of a paparazzo I recognize from LA. While he can be pushy, he's also harmless. And now, he's probably going to sue Beau for assault.

Beau's arm is thrown out, like the paparazzo is gunning for him.

A weird silence ripples over the growing crowd but all their phones are out, filming this moment to be watched by hundreds of thousands of people in seconds. No doubt Beau and I will become a series of memes.

Dread settles in my stomach. Partly for the backlash that is going to ensue but also for Beau's well-being. The genuine fear in his expression, followed by anger and rage, takes my breath away.

Was he here? In this moment? Or did his memories drag him back to Afghanistan and its darkness?

Strong arms pull me up and I look over my shoulder.

"I'm sorry, Celine. That guy came out of nowhere, posing as a customer," Caleb mutters, his mouth twisted in frustration, his eyes flashing. "Are you okay?"

"I'm fine." I brush my hands together as if it can shake off the moment.

"Get your hands off her, man," Beau demands.

"Beau," I say as I shake my head.

Beau snaps his neck toward the street where his truck is parked. "Let's go."

Caleb doesn't move. Instead, his presence looms over me, as if he doesn't trust Beau. While I want to scoff that it's ridiculous, I'd be lying if I didn't admit that for an instant, a heartbeat, Beau's anger frightened me.

"Beau!" Bea runs toward us.

Beau winces, as if the sight of his sister is painful, and she recoils. While I know it's his own embarrassment, his rebuff causes Bea to blanch. Brody appears and gives me a sympathetic glance.

"Y'all head home." Brody's tone is light and easy. He drops an arm around Bea's shoulders. "I'll call ya later."

Beau stalks off in the direction of his truck. Caleb successfully convinces the growing crowd to stop recording while the paparazzo spouts off at the mouth.

"You'll hear from my lawyer!" he shouts at Beau's retreating back. "Do you know how much this camera costs?"

I sigh, knowing I need to do damage control. My first call will be to Mellie who will relay the message to my publicist and her team. Not wanting to stick around to make the situation worse—although I don't know how much worse it can get at this point—I give Bea a quick squeeze and follow her brother.

He practically rips the passenger door off the hinges before he stalks to the driver's side and climbs in, quickly turning the engine.

"What was that?" I can't keep the accusation from my tone as I click in my buckle. Instantly, I regret it. It's not the best way to approach him when he's wound tight enough to snap. Beau glares at me and I gentle my tone. "Are you okay?"

He winces. "Are *you* okay?"

I frown, unable to read the man I used to know as well as myself. One glance, one casual remark, and I could read Beau's thoughts.

Now, I have no idea what's spinning in his mind.

"I'm fine," I say quietly.

He scoffs. Shaking his head at himself, he pulls out of the parking spot and points his truck in the direction of my place.

Instinctively, my hand wraps around the grab handle.

"You scared of me?" Beau asks, but his tone is hard. A thickly veiled edge of anger that causes the back of my neck to tingle in warning.

"You surprised me, Beau. I think you surprised everyone."

"He jumped out at us!"

"I know. It was sudden. And—"

"It's fucking unacceptable, Celine." Beau glances at me. "How the hell do you live like this?"

I shrug, not liking his tone but also wanting to understand his thoughts. I know his reaction is coming from a well of pain, from years of experiences I know very little about. I wish he would open up to me.

He turns his gaze back toward the road. "I'm gonna drop you off."

"And?" I prompt, wanting us to discuss this. Wanting him to let me in.

"And?"

"We should talk," I clarify, my own frustration rising. "You can't go around snapping at—"

"Don't tell me what I can and can't do," he bites out, not bothering to look at me.

"Beau, he's gonna sue you."

"He can do whatever the fuck he wants. As long as you're safe—"

"I wasn't in any danger," I tell him gently. "He just wanted a good picture. He was doing his job."

Beau's jaw tightens and ticks. "And I was doing mine! Trying to protect you, to defend you. How do you know he wasn't violent? That he wasn't going to put his hands on you?" His voice quivers with emotion. With *fear*. "The things I've seen…"

I wait for him to continue but he doesn't. We ride in charged silence for several moments.

"You can tell me," I say gently. "I want to know, Beau. What happened in Afghanistan? What keeps you up at night?"

He snorts but it's not amused. It's broken.

"I want to understand you," I press.

"Why?" He gives me a quick look, the corner of his mouth tugging upward. But it's more snarl than smirk. "You think you can fix me?"

"I never said that."

"Good. Realistic expectations." He pulls into my driveway.

The headlights of his truck light up the sweet little house, tucked into the country. I stare at it and wish my life was as simple and sweet as this place.

Beau moves the gear stick into park but doesn't turn off his truck.

"We need to talk," I say, my tone steely.

"You need to go," he refutes. "I fucked this up."

"You're hurting," I reply. "Let me in, Beau. Let me help you."

He shakes his head. "You can't. Celine, tonight was the tip of the iceberg. That guy's lucky all I did was break his camera. I wanted to fucking destroy him."

"For scaring you?"

"For threatening you," he replies.

"He wasn't threatening me. He was doing his job. I know

it's not cool all the time but our careers overlap. I'm doing my best to draw boundaries. I get that this transition has been tough for you. But I hate seeing you in pain, Beau. I hate seeing you in panic. I want to navigate this with you. Please, let me."

"This isn't the world I want to live in. You have no privacy in your life. No normalcy. Everything is a fucking spectacle. Everyone wants a piece of you. If you're always giving yourself to every fucking person in the world, what's left for those that love you?"

I start, taken aback by his words. "Beau—"

"I love you, Celine." He spits the words, his eyes wild. His fingers clench the steering wheel, his knuckles turning white. "But you belong to a world that I'll never fit into. You keep saying, this is my life. This is my career. We'll navigate it together. But we're not the same. You're capable of balancing this and I'm…" He gestures to himself. "I'm fucked up. I'm angry. I'm not capable of living the life that you love. That you strived to create. I messed up my sister's perfect night because my head is a fucking disaster zone. That's never going to go away."

"Beau…" I reach for him, place my hand on his knee. It trembles beneath my touch and my heart breaks. I roll my lips together, wanting to support him. Wanting him to know that I'm trying to understand his fears. The quick approach he didn't see coming, the flashing bulb, the defensive stance. "It's triggering," I murmur, recognizing the parts of my life that add stress to his. "Beau, I'm sorry."

He groans, dropping his head back against the headrest as his eyes close. Then, he moves forward so quickly, I gasp. My head thumps against the window behind me. Beau's eyes are filled with grief. "I'm not fixable, Celine. Why don't you get that? This"—he waves a hand in front of his chest—"isn't going to change. I fucking love you. I never stopped and I never will. But love isn't enough for people like me."

"What do you mean?" I practically wail, frustrated and hurt and thrilled by his declaration all at the same time. "I lo—"

"Don't say it," he cuts me off, his eyes pleading. "I'm not the same man I was. Don't you get that? You were fucking scared of me back there."

"I was caught off guard," I rationalize.

"I frightened you," he growls, his knuckles popping as he grips the steering wheel. "This is who I am now," he admits again, defeated. "I am no longer the right guy for you."

"Don't make decisions for me."

"Don't make excuses for me."

I keep my hand on his thigh, noting how it flexes under my touch. Beau stares straight ahead, refusing to meet my gaze.

"What if you talk to someone, Beau? There are professionals who can help you sort through this. There are—"

"You need to think about the life you want, Celine," he cuts me off. "Because I can't give you more than this. And I know this isn't nearly enough."

Tears well in my eyes as something deep inside cracks. Beau shatters me. I hate the pain he's wallowing in; I hate the suffering that produces shadows in his eyes.

"Come in," I beg. "I'll make us tea."

He shakes his head. "You should go. We should…take time."

"Time?"

"To think."

"What's there to think about? You just said you love me."

A sad smile flits over his face as his gaze—all heartbreak and hurt—flashes to mine. "Yeah. And that wasn't enough the first time. What makes you think it is now?"

"Beau," I repeat, trying to find the right words.

"Please, Celine. Go. Take some time. Think. I'm heading to Chicago for a game. Our lives, they don't mesh any more now than they did eight years ago. You need to recognize that."

I shake my head, refusing to accept his words, even though they're logical. But they don't line up with my feelings for him. They don't make sense to me. I scoff, my own temper flaring. "Fine." I pull my hand away from his leg. "You're right. You didn't fight for me then. Why the hell should I think you'd fight for me now?"

His eyes spark with anger. "Didn't fight for you?"

I shrug. "I never heard from you after I accepted the role in *Midnight Moon*. Where'd you go, Beau? What the fuck happened that made you cut ties with me completely?"

"I was going to propose to you!" he roars.

I jump at the animosity in his tone.

He snorts. "Yeah. I flew out to LA to fucking propose. And you made a choice that impacted both of our lives without even discussing it with me."

The resentment in his tone burns through me, leaving a trail of heat in my blood. "Was I supposed to? We were broken up. We—"

"I was still fucking in love with you," he snaps. "I am still fucking in love with you." Softer this time. "I thought things could be different. But, fuck, Celine, these past few weeks, we've been willfully ignorant."

At the defeat in his tone, my temper deflates. Coldness spread through my limbs. "I thought you were happy."

"Yeah. As happy as a man like me can be."

"What the hell does that mean?"

"It means that I'm not right for you, Cece. Less now than I was then. I didn't want to accept it. Hell, I fought it. I thought I could man up, be better, *change*. But that's not going to happen, and you need to accept it." He turns away from me again. Stares right at the little white bungalow with the rustic beams and porch. The kind of house he used to promise he'd build us. "Please"—his voice cracks—"go."

I glare at him. My emotions run into each other, vying for the top spot. Hurt, anger, guilt, resentment, surprise, desperation—all colliding in a violent crash that leaves me simultaneously hyped up and emotionally drained.

Without replying, I slip from his truck and slam the door as hard as I can. I see him flinch through the windshield and a little ripple of satisfaction runs through my chest.

Then, I stomp toward the porch and enter my home without a backward glance. I slam that door too and rest my back against it, breathing heavy in the darkness.

How the hell was I supposed to know Beau came to LA to propose? Is that why he cut ties with me? Because he felt rejected? Well, I fucking burned from his rejection.

Would I have accepted his proposal?

A trickle of unease drips down my spine and I feel simultaneously ashamed and vindicated. I flip on my living room lights.

Only then does Beau's truck back out of the driveway. I close the blinds, annoyed that he waited to make sure I turned on the lights before leaving. He may love me, but he doesn't want me—not enough to fight for me. This. Us.

His rejection hits differently the second time around. It cuts more than it burns. As an agonized sob climbs the walls of my throat, I drop to my knees and lower my head to the floor.

Then, I sob. For all the time Beau and I lost. For the way Beau views himself now.

For all the choices we made that led to this heartbreak.

Again.

TWENTY-THREE
BEAU

I BANG the end of my fist against the shower tile. Cold water rains down on my head and it does nothing to diffuse the heat moving through my blood stream like lava.

What the fuck was I thinking?

On the bathroom vanity, my phone lights up with another message.

I turn away from the glass of the shower door and close my eyes.

The messages haven't stopped. My teammates and siblings checking in on me. My coaches and agent inquiring what the fuck happened. Social media blowing up with everything from me being an entitled professional athlete who thinks I can put my hands on people to me being a victim of PTSD. There have been countless versions of the story, all bringing a slice of negative press to my sister's business venture. To Celine's career.

Guilt, shame, and humiliation burn through me in varying degrees.

What was I thinking? Why did I think I could make things work with Celine again? Our lives are more complicated than they were a decade ago and we couldn't figure shit out then either.

I finish showering and towel off. My phone continues to ping and light up with messages, but I ignore them. Instead, I clock the time, set an alarm, and force myself to pack.

Tomorrow, I'm flying to Chicago for a game. I need to get my head on straight. The thought of letting my team down—again—after embarrassing and hurting Celine—again—is a failure I can't accept.

I lay in bed for hours, praying for sleep to claim me. Of course, it doesn't. Instead, I'm plagued by images of Celine's dark eyes, brimming with sadness. The anger that flashed in them when she realized I was letting her go. The resentment in her tone when she hurled hurtful words at me.

You didn't fight for me then. Why the hell should I think you'd fight for me now?

Why can't she realize I let her go because that's what she wanted? Back then, her career ambitions trumped everything. If I proposed, we would have lived in two different countries as a newly married couple. It was never going to work.

And now? I'm fighting for an impossible outcome. Celine's world is too big, exciting, and complicated for mine.

I need stability. Simplicity. Home.

I turn onto my side and pull my covers up.

Home for me has always been Celine.

I flop onto my back, unable to get comfortable. Unable to silence the thoughts rolling through my mind.

It takes hours to find sleep and when it finally comes, it's filled with the torturous cries, the devastated sobs, the smoke and the lights and the noises from that night. Except Celine, with her heartache and pain, is in the center of it all.

"YOU LOOK LIKE SHIT," River comments as I slide into the seat behind him on the plane.

I ignore him and pull out my headphones.

"Sleep badly?" Axel guesses from the seat across the aisle.

I sigh and close my eyes.

"You gonna blow us all off?" Devon inquires, shoving past me into the window seat I purposely left empty in the hopes that no one would claim it.

River turns and stares down at me from the top of his seat. "You fucked that dude's camera."

"Jesus," I mutter, not in the mood for his shit. Or this conversation. Or any of the looks my teammates are pointing in my direction. "It was a mistake."

River shrugs. "He had it coming."

I narrow my eyes. "How can you be sure?" The entire night, I beat myself up. I know I crossed a line when I hit the paparazzo and broke his camera. Logically, I know I could have handled the situation better. While I am sorry for causing Celine, Bea, and Gran distress, I'm not sorry for putting that guy in his place.

"Dude, they've been hounding you and Celine for weeks. Anyone would've reacted by now." River turns around and slinks down in his seat.

"How's Celine?" Axel asks.

I swear again. "I guess she's good. I dropped her home last night."

"And?" Devon presses.

I glare at him. "Since when do you give a shit about gossip?"

"It's not gossip if one of my player's head's up his ass," he tosses back.

"What happened to the dick with the busted face?" River pipes up again.

I swear.

"He's fine. Pressing charges," Devon answers for me.

My head snaps toward his.

He shrugs. "It's public knowledge. He tweeted about it."

"Celine'll probably take care of it," River says. Possibly he means to reassure me, but all his words do is layer more stress on my shoulders.

The last thing I need is Celine cleaning up my mess. Haven't I already done enough? Caused her enough pain, created enough inconveniences in her life?

"You tried to end it with her," Axel correctly reads my mood and the situation.

"Bro, what the fuck?" River's face reappears on top of his seat. "Why the hell would you do that?"

Devon shrugs. "Couldn't man up?"

"Too much resentment," Axel deduces.

"Jesus, will y'all let me speak?" I blurt out.

River smirks. "You aren't saying shit."

I wipe my palm over my face. Grip the back of my neck. A tension headache wraps around my head. I swear again. "Look, not that I owe y'all an explanation, but things between Cece and me are complicated."

"Because of your past?" Axel prods.

"Cause she's a celebrity smoke show." River nods, as if he knows shit.

"Because I'm fucked in the head," I growl.

My teammates rear back and pause.

A heavy beat of silence passes. I fumble with my headphones, desperate to glue them to my ears and tune out this uncomfortable conversation.

"You're not." Damien leans over the side of my seat. I didn't realize he was sitting behind me and listening to the entire conversation. "You're hurting."

"You're confused," Axel agrees.

"You been through a lot," Devon decides.

"You should be in fucking therapy," River offers.

"That's what I keep telling him," Cole says, taking the aisle seat in front of Axel.

I glare at him.

Cole shrugs. "What? My therapist knows a great therapist."

"You're being too hard on yourself," Damien continues, as if the rest of the guys aren't offering their two cents. "And you're not giving Celine enough credit. If she wanted to cut ties with you, she would. She doesn't need your shit on top of her navigating a second shot with you."

"When did you become qualified at giving relationship advice?" Devon snorts.

Damien smirks. "Since Harper." He turns his gaze back to me. "And I've seen my brother deal with demons. Not the same as you, Turner. But I've watched him struggle enough to know that sometimes, we destroy the happiness we want because we're scared we won't be worthy of it. Don't destroy a good thing or a great woman because you don't think you're enough. You gotta fucking be enough."

"And how do I do that?" I try to quip, try to keep my tone light. Casual. But it lands heavy, the raw anguish in my voice giving away how twisted up over Celine I am.

River averts his gaze, as if my vulnerability is embarrassing. Hell, maybe it is.

But Damien doesn't back down. "Talk to her. Hear her out. And work through this shit." He flips his chin toward Cole. "Take Cole up on his offer. You can't try to beat on Brawler for the rest of your life."

I duck my head, hating that everyone knows about my sparring sessions with Axel.

"He can't beat me anyway," Axel remarks.

I flip him the middle finger.

He smiles which is always fucking scary since he doesn't do it often. "Barnes is right."

"Never thought I'd see the day," Devon mutters.

I arch an eyebrow, waiting for him to continue.

"When Damien Barnes would have something intelligent to say," Devon states.

Damien swears and I heave out a deep breath.

"You think I can salvage it?" I ask my teammates, as if they know the answer. As if their responses will somehow determine my fate with Celine.

But I hold my breath after I ask because it does matter. The fact that they're weighing in matters. After I lost the guys in my group—either from that night or the fallout that followed—there hasn't been anyone I could confide in. Rely on.

And now, the Bolts are stepping up in a way I never gave them credit for before.

As if he understands my thoughts on a deeper level, Damien smirks. "Only you know the answer to that, Turner. But, for what it's worth, she wouldn't have come back if it wasn't salvageable."

"She came for the movie," I remind him.

At that, all the guys surrounding me laugh.

Devon pats me on the head like I'm a fucking puppy. "Man up, Turner. Sooner rather than later. We got a game tonight."

The captain's voice comes over the intercom and my team-mates busy themselves with their tablets or headphones. I finally pull mine on and drown out the sounds of their move-ments with music.

A few minutes later, the plane moves down the runway.

By the time we hit cruising altitude, my eyes are closing. It's been a long night and an early morning. But my team-mates' words reassured something inside me. They've filled me with something that only Celine has managed to gift me in recent years.

Hope.

Maybe I can fix this. Maybe I can get better.

Maybe I'm capable of manning up and winning the woman after all.

"NICE GAME, TURNER!" Coach Scotch smacks my helmet as I skate off the ice.

We beat Chicago 2-1. While it wasn't my best performance, it was enough to secure a win and for that I'm grateful. The last thing I'd want is to let my teammates down after they willingly showed up for me.

"The charges against you were dropped," he adds in a lower tone.

I turn and give him a look.

He shrugs. "Just accept the support and go shower."

While I don't know the ins and outs of what went down to get the paparazzo to drop the charges, I let it go. Because clearly, people are intervening to step up for me. After years of being that guy for everyone else, I decide to accept the help.

Even if it makes me uncomfortable. Even if it goes against my nature. Because, I have a feeling, that I'm not going to get anywhere with Celine if I'm not open to accepting her support. Her concern.

Her unconditional love.

God, could she love me again? Now, with all the mistakes I've made and all that hurt I've caused?

I fucking hope so.

I shower quickly and step to my locker. The locker room chatter buzzes around me as I pull on a sweater and slacks. We're flying home tomorrow morning, and I can't wait. All I want to do is land in Tennessee, see Celine, and apologize for all the pain I've caused.

In twenty-four hours, my world flipped upside down.

I almost lost the woman of my dreams, again, because I was too wrapped up in my own shit to hear her out. I pushed her away because I'm embarrassed. Because I'm broken. Because I'm not the man I used to be.

But when has Celine ever given the impression that she doesn't want or care for this version of me?

The team is right; I need to let her. I need to give her my respect. I need to hear her out.

I just hope she gives me the time of day when I knock on her door. I hope she realizes that I want to fight for her, for us, more than anything else in the world. I just need a little help showing her how.

TWENTY-FOUR
CELINE

"YOU LOOK LIKE SHIT," I tell him when he pulls open the hotel door. He's wearing black slacks and a sweater. A light beard coats his cheeks. I smile. "And you look sexier than you have any right to."

Utter shock crosses Beau's face as he looks me up and down. "You're here."

I lean against the doorframe. "I'm here."

His expression crumples and he opens his arms. I step into them, fighting my tears as I bury my face in his chest.

"You're really here," he repeats, kissing the top of my head. "God, Celine. I'm so sorry. I'm so fucking sorry. I was going to come to your place the second I landed. I swear it."

I pull back to read his eyes. At the truth that swims in them, I hug him again. "I know. I couldn't sleep after the way things went down between us. I couldn't even think."

"Me neither," Beau agrees, ushering me into his hotel room.

When we're both inside, he sits me on the edge of the bed. He paces in front of me, his hands in his hair. "Are you hungry? Did you eat? When did you arrive?"

"I'm fine." I give him a little smile. "I came to your game. You were great."

"You did?" He rears back. "But…why?"

"Because it's my turn to fight for you, Beau. For us." It's only been a day and the thought of losing Beau, again, has wreaked havoc on my nervous system. My mind has been torn up over him, my emotions a jumbled mess, and my body more fatigued than it's felt in years. "I couldn't even get through shooting today. Thad covered for me, said I was sick. I bought a flight here, got a ticket for the game, and…" I shrug. "Here I am."

"Celine…" Beau drops to his knees by my side. He takes my hands in his, resting them on the tops of my thighs. His eyes are filled with regret, his expression twisted with anguish. "I'm sorry for not confiding in you when you asked me to," he starts. "I'm sorry for not including you in my life the way you begged me to." He rolls his lips together, as if to shore up his confidence. "I'm sorry for not trusting you the way I should. And for not respecting you to make your own decisions, without me sabotaging things to make the choice easier. Fuck, I'm sorry I failed you, Celine." He drops one of my hands to grip the back of his neck, pinch it tight. "I'm sorry I keep saying I'm fucking sorry. And I'm sorry I believed that my love, our love, wouldn't be enough for you." A shaky sigh. "Could it be?"

My heart shatters at the wavering hope threaded in his tone. He's too hesitant to trust it completely and still, he voices it for me to decide. Reaching for him, I pull him up to sit beside me on the bed. I turn into his frame, my hands wrapped around his arm. "You devastate me, Beau Turner."

He frowns.

I smirk. "From the first moment I laid eyes on you, you've wrecked me."

His arm wraps around my back. He holds me close. Steady and soothing, just like I remember.

"I've never not wanted you. Or this." I snuggle into his side, shift so I can watch his expression. "I just wanted other things too. Alongside our relationship. It was never an either/or. It was always an *and*. You decided otherwise."

"I felt like you chose your career over us," he admits. "I thought the distance and the missing would turn to resentment. We wouldn't support each other the way we're supposed to but hold each other back instead."

"Yeah," I say, understanding why he made the choices he did nearly a decade ago. "But how did it work out anyway? We didn't talk for eight years, Beau."

"And I missed you the whole time."

I smile. "Me too. You said it the other night; now it's my turn. I never stopped loving you, Beau. I never stopped wanting you. I never moved past what we shared, not in any way that counts. And I want this with you but you've gotta let me in. You have to trust me. And you have to start trusting yourself by getting the support you need to heal."

His face twists in anguish so raw it steals my breath.

"You're carrying around too much. Too many wounds. Too much hurt. Blame. Guilt." I lean into him. "You need to share the load, Beau. All I've ever wanted was for you to share it with me."

"Back then, I thought you'd leave," he admits.

"I left anyway," I remind him. "If we want this to work, we need to work for it."

"I know. I want to be the man I should have been back then."

"I wasn't ready for him," I admit sadly. "But I am now. I choose you. I choose us." I let out an exhale. "You need to speak to a professional, Beau. Work on your PTSD."

He pulls back and I tighten my hold.

"Not for me, or us," I continue, "but for you. Beau, you need support."

"I have you. My brothers and Bea. Gran."

I shake my head sadly. "You won't let any of us in the way you need to. And that's okay; it doesn't have to be one of us. Maybe a stranger, a therapist, will be a better choice. What's the harm in trying?"

"Cece."

"Please, Beau. Please."

"I love you, Celine." He drops his forehead to mine, and I close my eyes, breathing in his scent, holding his presence in my heart.

"I love you too."

He tucks a finger under my chin and lifts my face to his. Staring into my eyes, he slowly nods. "For you, I will." Then, he dips his face and we kiss.

It's reverent. Filled with emotion, lined with old hurts and new longings. I tip forward, my arms encircling Beau's neck as he holds me tighter, flush against his chest. His arm wraps around my lower back like a band, keeping me pressed against him.

I part my lips and his tongue delves inside, stroking mine with long, meaningful movements. Our kiss burns through me, passionate and heady. He pauses, breaks our kiss to pull off his sweater as I remove mine.

We undress quickly, our clothing and shoes lying in a discarded pile on the floor.

While I remain seated on the edge of the bed, Beau stands before me, already hard, pitching an impressive tent in his boxer briefs. Wanting to see all of him, I tug on the band of his boxer briefs and pull them down. He springs free and I wrap my hand around the shaft, working him slowly.

He watches, a little in awe, as if he can't believe the turn of events. His hand buries in my hair, his fingers gripping.

His cock weeps one bead of precum and my tongue darts out to lap it up. Beau groans, both hands clutching my hair. I look up at him, noting how hooded his eyes are. They're dark with desire and swirling with need. I keep my eyes glued to his as I part my thighs, shift my ass to the edge of the bed, and take him in my mouth.

Beau's grip on my hair tightens and a guttural groan falls from his throat, needy and so sexy I feel my own pleasure pulse. I grip the base of his shaft and work my hand and mouth in tandem, reveling in the sounds Beau makes, loving how his quads tighten.

"Celine…" His voice cracks as he pulls me up. Standing before him, he kisses me hard before laying me down in the center of the bed and hovering over me. I'm clad in a see-through lace bralette with matching panties and Beau's hands skim over the delicate lace, touching me so lightly that every nerve ending in my body zaps to life. He kisses the side of my neck, his fingertips gliding over my breasts, teasing my nipples into points. Then his mouth is moving over the lace cups, sucking my nipples through the lace, providing a delicious friction that has me arching my breast into his mouth, desperate for more attention.

He gives it freely, his other hand dipping in between my thighs. Beau strokes me there, hooking my panties to the side to drag his fingers through my folds. "You want me?"

"Always," I manage before his thumb applies pressure to my clit. "Beau." My hips buck up.

"Need you, Celine." He rolls down my body and then, his mouth replaces his fingers, tasting me through the lace my panties.

"Oh God," I moan, looking down to watch him as he licks up my arousal like it's his favorite dessert. "Beau." His hand travels up my curves, pulling down my bralette to fasten over my breast. His fingers play with my nipple and his tongue dips inside my most sensitive spot. My pleasure builds, slowly at first, and then, an uncontrollable need. "Beau, you're going to make me come."

"Then come," he commands. And I do, breaking apart under his mouth, his hands, his watchful gaze.

Before I come down completely, he moves again and pushes inside me, his cock stretching my walls as I cling to him. "You feel so good, Celine. Like fucking home," he mutters before slowly dragging out.

He's rock hard and wanting and my body hasn't recovered from my first orgasm before the second one starts.

Beau brushes my hair away from my face and gazes longingly into my eyes as he sets a torturously slow, but delicious, pace that has us both breathing raggedly. He makes love to me with intention in his movements, with apologies spilling from his eyes.

It's honest and raw. It's open and communicative. It's the most beautiful and heartbreaking connection of my life.

"I love you, Celine," he whispers before he falls over the edge, filling me with his want for me.

"I love you, Beau." I hold him closer, keeping him inside as he gathers me against his chest and rolls to his side.

We stay like that, connected in every way possible, losing ourselves in each other's gazes as we come down from the most intoxicating moment of my life. I feel lovestruck.

"We have to do better," Beau murmurs.

"We have to let go of the past. Start fresh," I reply.

He kisses the tip of my nose. "I choose you, Celine. I want this. I want *you*. I'm going to get help. I'll figure out how to navigate your world, how to live with less privacy in mine."

"Oh, Beau," I sigh. "I'm going to set more boundaries too. We'll figure out something that works for both of us, for both of our careers. We just need to be honest with each other and communicate."

"You're right."

I smile and brush my lips over his. "Good. Because I want you too, Beau."

His eyes lighten and a smile flits over his mouth. Then, he kisses me again. Deeply, passionately, intentionally. I feel him begin to harden inside of me and I flatten my palms against his shoulders, urging him closer.

Beau makes love to me again and I drown in his riptide, losing all sense of time. Instead, I fall into my future with him, filled with hope for what will come.

Then, we both drift to sleep, wrapped up in the comfort of each other and the knowledge that our future is intertwined.

TWENTY-FIVE
BEAU

"HAPPY FRIENDSGIVING!" Mila Lewis raises her wine glass.

"To chosen families," Damien adds, surprising everyone at the table.

Harper flashes him a smile and he grins back, looking nothing like the aloof ladies' man I met over a year ago. As Celine raises her glass beside me, I understand Damien's transformation. Celine re-entering my life has had a profound impact in a short amount of time.

I raise my beer. "To the Bolts."

"To the Bolts," everyone echoes.

We all take a drink of our beverages. Devon stands at the head of the table. "You want to see a real man carve a fucking turkey?" He picks up a carving knife.

"Yes," Axel interjects, standing beside him and taking the knife from his hand. "We all do. Sit down, city boy, before you lose a finger."

Devon scowls before snickering good-naturedly. Axel carves up the turkey. Mila and Maisy crack up. Harper shakes her head and begins dishing out salad. Celine reaches for the marshmallow yams and adds some to my plate before serving herself.

Cole catches my eye and gives me a knowing look while my sister practically melts beside him. And I get it. Their happiness. The energy around the table. The genuine joy, the deep sincerity, the satisfaction of *knowing*. Knowing that you're loved, that you're enough, that you're here, in this moment, with good people.

I smile at my sister and place a hand on Celine's lower back. I breathe in the moment and savor it because I haven't felt this at peace in years.

River Patton shadows the doorway of Damien's dining room in his ridiculous penthouse. Surveying the table, the corners of his mouth turn up when he notes that Lola Daire is present and that the only empty chair is beside her.

Internally, I groan. River Patton has a reputation, and it isn't one Axel wants his baby girl tangling up with. Luckily, Axel is fixated on perfecting his turkey-carving responsibilities. The fact that Maisy shoots River a warning look provides enough relief that I turn my attention toward Celine.

"You happy?" she asks.

I nod. "I'm thankful for you," I tell her, unprompted.

She grins. "You still do that?"

"We still do that," Bea responds. Turning toward Cole and the table at large, she explains, "We need to go around and say the thing we're most thankful for this year." Her eyes cut back to me. "You can start, Beau."

When all the eyes swing toward me, I dip my head, embarrassed by the attention.

"Isn't it obvious?" Damien asks. "He's thankful Celine gave his sorry ass a second chance and—"

"I'm thankful for Celine," I agree, cutting him off and slipping my hand into my woman's.

She squeezes. "And I'm thankful that Beau and I got a second chance. It's not always the case, so we're lucky."

"Aww." Maisy presses a palm to her chest, the solitaire engagement ring on her finger glistening. "I'm thankful—"

"That you're marrying Brawler," Damien supplies.

Axel glares at him. "You gonna let my woman talk?"

Damien holds up his hands in apology. "Sorry, Mais."

Maisy shrugs and looks at Axel, a small smile playing over her lips. "It's okay. I am thankful to marry Axel." Her eyes swing around the table, and she rolls her lips together, excited. "We're getting married June 22nd!"

"Yes!" Mila fist pumps. "Finally, a date! Oh my God, I can't wait. I'm thankful to be this chick's maid of honor!"

"Oh my gosh." Maisy laughs. "Of course." She reaches over the table to hug her best friend. "I'm so excited!"

"Same," Lola cuts in, her eyes darting between the best friends. "Dress shopping?"

"So much shopping," Mila gushes.

Axel clears his throat. "I'm grateful for family." His arms widen to encircle Maisy and Lola.

Lola rolls her eyes but grins. "I'm thankful to finally be a senior."

"How's that going?" Bea asks her.

She shrugs. "All good. I'm starting to put out some feelers for jobs." Her eyes slide to her dad and she wrinkles her nose. "The big guy doesn't want to admit it but—"

Axel's hand covers Lola's mouth to silence her. "We don't need to talk about California now."

"Ahh, yeah!" Devon says, enthusiastically. "After New York, California is the shit. Silicon Valley?"

Lola smiles and nods. Axel scowls.

"Uh," Harper cuts in. "I'm thankful to live back in Tennessee, but with a life."

"You're welcome," Damien adds.

Everyone rolls their eyes.

"I'm thankful for forgiveness," he adds, catching everyone by surprise again.

As the team stares at him, he clears his throat loudly and Cole speaks up.

"I'm thankful for stability." His hand covers my sister's, and she flips her palm to interlace their fingers.

"And I'm thankful for all the support in my life. Thank you all for coming to check out Humble Bee's," Bea adds.

A few people ask Bea about her new store. Then, silence descends as everyone's eyes swing toward Devon and River.

Devon lifts an eyebrow and River heaves out a sigh, as if he can't find anything worthwhile to be thankful for.

"I'm thankful to be here," he mutters, showing more emotion than usual. His eyes are glued to Lola when he says it and this time, Axel catches on and tosses a menacing look River's way.

Devon opens his mouth and draws the table's attention. "I'm thankful for all of you. This team we built from the ground up, the family we formed." He lifts his glass. "Happy Thanksgiving, Thunderbolts."

Again, we cheers. Then, we dive in and eat one hell of a feast, surrounded by love and laughter and *knowing*.

MY HANDS FEEL clammy as I knock on the door to the therapist's office.

He opens it immediately, a warm smile cutting his face. "Captain Turner."

I shake his hand. "Sir. It's good to meet you."

"Call me Brad. Come on in." He holds the door wider.

I step inside Brad's office and glance around. I don't know what I'm expecting but it isn't the comfortable, clean office space with oversized navy chairs and an amoeba-shaped oak coffee table.

"Take a seat wherever you'd like," Brad says, folding himself into one of the armchairs.

I look around for the chaise lounge and snort when I don't see one. Instead, I take the seat opposite his.

"You can start whenever you're ready. Why don't you tell me about yourself? About what led to your decision to come in today."

I rake my palms over my jeans, try to shake off my nerves. *Cole's therapist Cassie suggested I sit down with Brad. Cole trusts Cassie's judgement. Celine thinks this is a good idea. Bea's been encouraging me for nearly two years to seek out a therapist.*

The responses flit around my mind. I open my mouth. "I don't want to feel on edge all the time."

Brad's expression doesn't change. I don't know why I expected him, a therapist, to be shocked by my confession. Instead, he leans back in his chair and crosses one ankle over the opposite knee. "What do you mean by on edge?"

I clear my throat. "Anxious. Nervous. Quick to anger, quick to react."

Brad nods. "Do those emotional responses exacerbate in certain situations?"

I think back to the last few months with Celine. The not knowing. Her safety. Paparazzi. I nod. Then, I open my mouth to tell Brad about Celine's career.

But those words don't fall out. Instead, I hear myself telling him about the dreams. About the screams and cries and the permanent stench of fear.

Instead, I tell him about Afghanistan.

"HOW'D IT GO?" Cole asks as I leave Brad's office an hour later.

I shake my head at my teammate who is now more like

family. Another brother. "You didn't have to drop me off and wait around."

"I wanted to. You hungry?"

"Sure," I agree, falling into step with Cole as we walk to the parking lot.

He takes a swig of some green juice he's drinking, draining the bottle before tossing it into a trash can.

"It went well," I answer his question.

"Not awkward?"

I shake my head. "Surprisingly, not awkward at all. Brad served."

"Yeah," Cole agrees. "That's what Cassie said." He glances at me. "I'm glad you went, Beau."

"Yeah." I heave out a sigh, smacking Cole on the shoulder. "Me too."

"Stick with it, okay? Even after you think things are better. Stick with it for a while." He glances at me from the corner of his eye. "It can help in more ways than you think."

I look at Cole and nod once before opening the passenger door to his car. I slip inside and pull on my seat belt. Cole does the same, flipping the ignition, and pointing his car in the direction of The Rib Shack.

We're silent during the ride, both of us lost in our thoughts. But I feel calmer, more settled, than I did this morning. I know my family and the team have been worried about me. I know I pushed Celine away. I know I'm not the same guy I was before I enlisted.

But right now, I feel like myself again. When I look at Cole, I see more than a teammate, but a friend. A brother. And I'm grateful that he's the guy looking out for my sister.

We pick up a huge takeout order from The Rib Shack before heading to Gran's house. When we get there, my brothers are hanging out on the front porch.

"Hey!" Bodhi calls out. "How'd it go?"

"Not bad," I reply.

Brody slaps my shoulder and takes two takeout trays from my hands. "Hungry?"

"I can eat," I say.

"Hurry up," Blake says from the porch, glancing over his shoulder. "We left Gran alone with the Silver Fox and I'm not sure what they're up to."

Bodhi and Cole groan. Blake laughs.

I shake my head and follow the guys into Gran's house. Bea's seated at the table with Celine, the two of them having tea and catching up like old times.

Gran's laughter wafts through the house, followed by the Silver Fox's chuckle. I help Bea set the table and then, we all sit down for a family lunch.

It feels right, natural. All the awkward tension from before has eased and in its place is the peace I've been searching for.

I know I've got my work cut out for me. I know everything isn't magically better now. But it's a step in the right direction. As I look around the table, taking in my siblings' smiling faces, hearing Gran's hilarious quips, reveling in Celine's boisterous laughter, I'm filled with gratitude.

This year, I'm thankful to be home.

TWENTY-SIX
CELINE

"THAT'S A WRAP!" the director calls out.

The entire cast and crew, everyone on set who contributed to this film's completion, claps and cheers.

Thad brushes a kiss over my temple. "You're a true star, Celine. I wish I could film every movie with you."

I laugh and wrap my arm around his waist, giving him a side hug. "We did good."

"Oscar good?"

I bite my bottom lip and squeal. "I sure hope so!"

"Get them a drink!" one of our costars calls out.

A moment later, Mellie passes Thad and me flutes of champagne and we all cheers to the success of the film we completed.

When I step off set, strong arms wrap around me, holding me close for a long moment.

"You were incredible," Beau murmurs into my hair.

I pull back and beam up at him. "I can't believe it's over."

He shakes his head. "It's just beginning, baby."

I snort. "You know what I mean." Turning in his arms, I settle against Beau's strong frame. His arms wrap around my middle, his fingers playing with the fringe along the bottom of my shirt.

"We going out to celebrate?" he murmurs.

I nod. "Thad made reservations at Strickland's."

"Fancy," Beau agrees. It's where he took me on our first big date at the start of senior year. He worked all summer to save up for dinner at the best steakhouse in Knoxville.

"Tomorrow night, me and you, dinner at my place?" I ask him.

"Wouldn't miss it," he says easily. "But don't go crazy. I have a game—"

"The day after. I know," I say. "I'll be there."

"In my jersey?"

"Always in your number," I agree.

He grins and kisses my cheek before releasing me. Some of the crew approach and I'm swept into the celebrations.

I came to Tennessee to film a movie. At least, that's what I told myself. I really came to Tennessee to see about Beau. When I saw him in April, at Gran's party, I knew there was unfinished business between us.

Now, when I look at him, I know his love is it for me. Beau Turner has always been the man of my dreams come true. Now, he's my future. I just have to tell him.

I PULL open the door to my house when Beau's boots hit the porch.

He lifts his eyebrows. "Waiting for me?"

"Always." I step outside to greet him.

He reaches for me, tugging me close and planting a hard kiss on my mouth. "Missed you today."

"How was therapy?"

"Good." His eyes are clearer when he says it and I know

he's making great strides. It's only been three weeks since Beau started and already, I see a difference in him. A few days ago, he admitted he doesn't reach for his anxiety pills as much. It's progress.

I think the work he's doing is filling him with a quiet confidence and restoring his ability to trust his decisions. As such, his play on the ice has improved. His interactions with his family have been more open and playful.

And his relationship with me? Well, it's as sweet and thrilling as I remember.

"I made mac and cheese for dinner," I tell him as we step inside my home.

He groans appreciatively. "Smells delicious. So much for eating light."

"You said don't go crazy. Mac and cheese isn't crazy."

Beau swats at my ass. "And for dessert?"

I spin around and laugh. "My bedroom?"

"Now you're talking, Cece." He takes my hand and guides me toward my bedroom. "We could do an appetizer too, you know."

I laugh and follow along. No way am I denying the opportunity to get naked with this man.

Beau turns toward me before sitting on the edge of my bed. His hands palm the back of my thighs as he pulls me closer and rests his cheek against my belly. I run my fingers through his hair.

"Thank you," he says, glancing up at me.

I shake my head. "For what?"

"Not giving up on me. Fighting for us. Convincing me to see Brad."

"That's all you," I remind him. Beau working through things to help himself heal is a huge deal and he should get the credit for the hard work he's putting in.

"I love you, Cece. More than you can possibly imagine."

I drop my face to his. Give his lips a long, lingering kiss. "I love you too. I got something for you. For us."

He smiles. "What is it?"

I shimmy out of his hold to spread my arms wide. "Welcome home."

Beau's eyebrows bend together as he glances around my room. "What?"

"I bought the Klingers' place."

Wonder ripples over his expression and a surprised laugh tumbles from his mouth. "You bought this house?"

"It's our little country retreat," I say, spinning around the room.

Beau catches me, his hands finding my hips as he stands before me. "You bought us a house?"

I nod. "Honestly, I was going to buy it no matter what. I like the way I feel when I'm here. I like the peace this place brings me. But more than that, I love being here with you. Right now, I have to go back to LA and do my best to split my time between California and Tennessee. You're traveling a lot with the team. At least now, we have a place we can retreat to. A spot that's quiet and secluded and just ours."

Beau shakes his head, his eyes brimming with emotion. "Our hideaway?"

"Exactly."

He kisses the tip of my nose before his thumb slips under my chin and he angles my face to kiss my mouth. Long, deep, and passionately. "I want to hide away with you forever, Celine." His lips move over mine.

I smile. "Can we start now?"

"We already started."

I laugh as Beau picks me up and drops me in the center of my bed. Then, he shows me how much he loves me and how much he wants me. Beau Turner gifts me the homecoming I've craved, and I savor every second of it.

Afterwards, we sit on my back porch, huddled close

together and wrapped in plaid blankets. We watch the sunset, listen to the crickets, and share a big bowl of macaroni and cheese.

It's simple and effortless.

It's everything I've always wanted.

EPILOGUE

BEAU

CELINE'S EYES twinkle and she clasps her hands together in excitement as I haul the oversized Christmas tree into the living room with Cole's help.

"Did you really cut it down?"

"We had one hell of a job cut out for us," I reply.

She laughs. "It's huge!"

"You should see the one at Gran's house," Cole replies as we heave the tree into the stand.

"So much decorating to do," Celine announces, disappearing into her bedroom and returning with an exorbitant number of shopping bags.

"Wow," Cole whispers. "This is intense."

"Tell me about it," I agree.

"My family arrives in three days, Beau. We have so much to do," Celine says. She begins pulling boxes of Christmas ornaments from the boxes. "Wait till you see what I got for the top of the tree."

"A star?" Cole guesses.

"Better," Celine replies, digging around in the bag. She pulls out a giant thunderbolt and Cole and I crack up.

"Where did you even find that?" I ask.

She shrugs. "Something to do with a DC Comics themed Christmas tree and Shazam."

"The lightning bolt," Cole agrees.

Celine shrugs. "Looks like thunder to me."

"It will look perfect on the top of our tree," I reassure her, moving closer to kiss the top of her head.

While this isn't the first Christmas I've spent outside of Gran's home, it's the first time I care about a tree and ornaments and making a home feel like Christmas.

It feels like the first holiday season since I was a kid that I'm filled with excitement and happiness to share a meal, to hang a wreath on the front door, to wrap presents.

"I'll catch you guys later," Cole says, brushing pine needles off his palms.

"Thanks for your help, Cole." Celine moves closer to hug him good-bye. "We're hosting a New Year's Eve party, spread the word."

Cole glances at me and I shrug. This is news to me.

Celine smiles. "My movie wrapped. I've got downtime and I want to spend it here, ringing in the new year with y'all."

I tuck her under my arm and kiss her upturned lips. "Then that's what we'll do." I look at Cole. "Spread the word."

"I'm on it," he agrees, grinning at us like we're puppies. "See you tomorrow, Beau."

"Later." I walk him out.

Once I close the door and turn around, I groan.

Celine stands before me with armfuls of string lights. She passes them over and grins. "Get to work, Turner. I know you've got a toolbox in that truck."

"I like doing Christmas with you, Cece," I say truthfully, taking the rolls of lights from her.

"I like doing everything with you, Beau. And"—she

pauses and wrinkles her nose—"there's a massive wreath and more shopping bags in the hall closet."

I snort. "How long have you been hoarding Christmas decorations?"

She shrugs. "Every time you have an away game, Harper and I have been hitting the outlets. There are a lot of holiday themed sales happening."

"Of course there are," I mutter, moving toward the porch. But I'm happy Celine and Harper clicked. I love that she's spending time with the Bolts girls, making friends, and reestablishing a home base in Tennessee. With me.

Celine and I spend the evening decorating our hideaway for the holidays. Then, we spend a week hosting our families and friends for dinners, drinks, and a slew of celebrations.

When we collapse into our bed on January 1, I turn toward my everything and kiss her hard. "Happy New Year, baby."

"Happy everything, Beau." She snuggles closer and presses her mouth to the base of my throat. "It's going to be a good year."

"The best," I agree. Knowing I get to drift off to sleep with Celine in my arms already makes this the best New Year's of the last decade. The knowing that we're going to face our challenges—careers, distance, busy schedules—together makes all the difference.

This time, I trust myself. I trust Celine.

This time, I have the utmost trust in *us*, and I know we're finally home.

THANK you so much for reading *Hero's Risk*! I hope you rooted for and fell in love Beau and Celine! Want to read what they're up to a year in the future? Grab the bonus epilogue here.

DESPERATE FOR THE final book in the Tennessee Thunderbolts series? Read *Bad Boy's Downfall* now. Turn the page to dive in!

BAD BOY'S DOWNFALL

CHAPTER ONE - RIVER

Lola Daire shouldn't be hot.

I mean, she wears shapeless dresses that hide her figure. Or fucking overalls.

Her nose is usually in a book, her face often devoid of makeup, and sometimes, I wonder if she's living in reality or in her own head. She's always thinking, caught up in her thoughts or brimming with ideas and possibilities.

By normal standards, she's quirky, at best. She shouldn't be hot.

By my standards, she's the most gorgeous woman I've ever laid eyes on. It's annoying. Distracting. Infuriating.

"Can you pass the potatoes?" she asks.

I heave out a sigh like reaching across the table is a big inconvenience but it's not. I just hate the way her father, my teammate, Axel Daire, also known as Brawler, shoots me dirty looks for talking to his precious kid. Ever since I sat down at this Friendsgiving dinner, I've been on the receiving end of Axel's glares, or his fiancée and my fucking friend Maisy's warning glances. I pass Lola the stupid potatoes.

Our fingers brush and even though I know I should pull

back, I don't. Instead, I hook my index finger over her middle one and hold for a moment too long.

Her chocolate eyes pierce mine, sparking with surprise and curiosity.

I flash a wicked smirk before releasing my hold. Of course, she's curious; she's a bookworm. Founder of a "girls who code" club on UT's campus. Her curiosity is insatiable, and I like that I intrigue her.

"Thanks," she murmurs.

I dip my head and turn my focus back to my plate. The turkey and mashed potatoes remind me of Gayle's Thanksgiving dinners. All homemade pies and cloth napkins, good wine and football in the background.

My foster parents are good people, hell, they took me in and put me on a better life path when I was floundering. Even though I'm missing Thanksgiving this year since the Bolts have an away game, I'll swing by next week to visit with Gayle. Although I can never give her what she really wants—a loving and forthcoming son—I can make conversation for an hour over coffee cake in her cozy kitchen.

"Who needs another drink?" Damien asks, standing from the table.

Our team captain, Devon, holds up his nearly drained bottle. Maisy grins and says she'll take another. Harper, Damien's woman, stands to help him as more teammates call out drink orders.

When Lola begins to add her order, her father clamps a hand over hers and gives her a stern look. "You're driving," he mutters.

She drops her head and I fucking hate that he won't let her loosen up and have a good time. She's with his team—with him—for fuck's sake. What does he think is going to happen? She can't get into any trouble here. Besides, I'd be happy to give Lola a ride home.

I drop a hand to her thigh under the table, give a reassuring squeeze. Her eyes jump to mine, shocked. A spark flares to life in my gut. Her surprise encourages my bad behavior. Even though it's stupid, messing with her feels good. Her reactions kick-start responses in me that feel half like memories.

Wanting, yearning, desiring. But more than a quick fuck. More than a fleeting moment.

Shit. What is wrong with me? I pull my hand from her thigh, the heat of her skin seeping through her jeans and into my fingertips as I remove my touch.

She's completely out of my league, the kind of girl that would never look at me. The type of woman who knows, with one glance, that she's too good for the type of bullshit I flip. But hell if I can't stop thinking about her.

It's been a year and a half since I met Lola. She signed her dad and herself up to be part of the welcome committee as the Thunderbolts team formed and players from out of state arrived.

Since I've been living in Tennessee for years now, having come up through the developmental league and being part of a feeder program to secure my spot with the Bolts, Lola had asked if I wanted to volunteer to greet players.

I scoffed and shut that shit down real fast. Since Lola's smart, she kept her distance. But over the course of the past year, something shifted. I'd catch her out with her friend Jasmine, grabbing drinks at Corks, and we'd chat. I made her laugh twice at Maisy and Axel's engagement party. When I came down with the flu in September, she dropped off a care package on my doorstep. It was the only time I've had a woman, save for Gayle, try to take care of me and it felt as good as it was unsettling.

Because, as the guys I grew up with would quickly point out, I've got no shot with her.

Damien and Harper return with another round of drinks and my teammates start to push away from the table, too full to keep eating. Little pockets of conversation break out, clustered in groups around the kitchen and living room.

Brawler and Maisy join Turner and his Hollywood-famous girlfriend Celine near the fireplace. Without her father's presence, Lola gives me a long look.

I stare back, waiting for her to tell me to knock it off or stop screwing around with her. She doesn't.

I let out an exhale. "Excited for senior year?"

She smiles. "Yeah, it's hard to believe I'm graduating this year."

"And you're thinking about moving to California?" I ask, even though I'm just repeating things she mentioned to Devon earlier.

"Silicon Valley has a ton of great IT and tech jobs," she explains.

"So does Texas," I toss out, recalling something my brother Cullen recently mentioned.

A dash of surprise darts over Lola's face. "You're right. I'm keeping my options open, casting a wide net."

"But you don't want to stay here?" I press, wanting to know that she's leaving. Wanting to know that she's got a big, bright future away from here.

Lola shrugs, glancing around Damien's penthouse. "It's not that I don't want to stay more than I want to know what other options exist. My mom and stepdad, my brothers, are in Seattle."

"Right." I nod.

"Your family's local, right?" she asks, turning the tables.

I drop my chin. I hate talking about my family. Not because I don't care and admire them for taking me in, but because I've never truly felt like I belonged. How could I? Gayle and Ken are those parents you see in movies, the types who should win awards for being so damn generous. They already had a son, Cullen, when I entered their lives. Still, they gave me every opportunity they gave him, including their unconditional support. Their love.

I never deserved it. I never earned it. Hell, half the time I was too angry to fucking appreciate it.

I clear my throat. "Yeah."

"That's nice," Lola says. "It's always good to be near family." Her eyes cross the space to snag on her dad and Maisy. "I'll miss them if I leave."

I clear my throat again, feeling like something is clogging it. I tug at the collar of my crewneck. I've seen enough of the relationship between Axel and Lola to know that they're close.

That Axel will come for me in my fucking sleep if I make a pass at his daughter.

Lola glances at me, her midnight eyes drawing me in. She flips her hair over her shoulder, and I notice, not for the first time, how silky it is. While she inherited her dark eyes and hair from her father, her petite stature and delicate bone structure must be from her mom. "Do you have any plans for the holidays?"

I take a swig of my beer. "Not really. I'll visit with my family, catch up with some friends, and that's about it. You?"

She frowns at my half-assed answer, but I'm not used to this, confiding and sharing. I'm cool with the team but only as deep as I'm willing to go. I don't overshare like the Rookie or give my two-fucking-cents like Damien Barnes. I'm more like Turner, but not as polite or genuine.

"I'm going to Seattle. I haven't seen my mom since summer, and I miss her. Besides"—her gaze skates over her dad again, her expression wistful—"my dad and Maisy should have some time to themselves, without me blowing up their spot."

I tilt my head, considering her words. Out of everyone I've met through the Thunderbolts, save for Lola, I like Maisy best. As much as Lola and Maisy click, I guess it would be weird to see her dad date and develop a relationship.

"Too bad," I mutter.

She glances at me.

"If you were staying in town, I was going to see if you wanted to kick it over winter break," I toss out, testing the waters.

Lola smirks and gives me a little shove. "No, you weren't."

I snort. "I was," I swear, even though it sounds like bullshit.

She rolls her eyes. "Yeah right."

I shake my head. "Why do you think I wouldn't want to hang with you?"

She sobers, her eyes growing serious. "Because I'm nothing like you, River." She gestures toward the living room where the Bolts players and their significant others are hanging out. "You belong to this, this world." She shrugs. "And...I don't really fit in."

I stare at her for a long beat before nodding in understanding.

Even though Lola isn't saying anything I don't know, the resignation in her tone gives me pause. But she's right; we belong to two separate worlds. In fact, they're so far apart they shouldn't even be in the same solar system.

But she's also wrong. Lola Daire could fit in anywhere; it's me who's lacking.

It always has been.

CHAPTER TWO - LOLA

My heart rate picks up when River Patton walks through the door.

"You came!" Maisy exclaims, enveloping him in a hug.

My dad's jawline tightens, and I try not to laugh.

Dad meets my gaze and gives me a look. I smile back and he sighs, gripping the back of his neck in frustration.

My father adores his fiancée, Maisy. I do too. She's a blessing in both of our lives and family. But he can't stand that she has a genuine friendship with the player on his team that irks him the most: River Patton.

Thank God he doesn't know that I also harbor a soft spot for the right-winger. Except my soft spot isn't wrapped in a maternal nurturing like Maisy.

I have a massive crush on River that is as mortifying as it is thrilling. Right now, I'm flustered and delighted that he's attending the Bolts Christmas gathering Dad and Maisy are hosting before I leave for Seattle.

"What can I get you to drink?" Maisy asks River after taking his coat.

"Don't worry about me, Mais," he says easily. He's comfortable with Maisy in a way that he isn't with most of the team. Less closed off. "I'll grab a beer." He gestures toward the kitchen.

"Damien and Devon haven't left the kitchen island," Maisy points out, glancing toward the two men who are standing by the food in the open concept kitchen.

River snickers. "You got ribs, didn't you?"

"The Rib Shack," Maisy confirms.

River approaches my dad and sticks out a hand, his eyes cutting to me for a flash before they focus on my father. "How's it going, Axel?"

"Fine," Dad replies. At Maisy's look, he sighs. "You?"

A smirk plays around River's mouth as his eyes find mine again. "All right."

Dad nods. River heads into the kitchen. Maisy pulls Dad into a conversation with Cole and Bea.

I try to get a handle on my erratic emotions. It's stupid; River Patton doesn't see me as anything but a kid, the way all my dad's teammates do.

The thought rings false. There's *something* with River; I just can't put my finger on it. Is it because we're nearly the same age? Or because we're the only two single people at the Bolts events these days? But whenever we talk, there's a spark. There's a lick of desire and a thrill of excitement that doesn't exist when Devon asks me about moving to California or Cole inquires if I need extra hockey tickets for my sorority sisters.

Things with River are just *different*.

I roll my lips together. My phone buzzes in the back pocket of my jeans and I pull it out.

JAS

Sorry, babe. I got called into work so I can't make today's soiree. See you tonight? X

Damn. If Jasmine can't come, that means I'll end up sleeping at Dad's tonight since I'm planning to drink some wine. It also means River and I are the only unattached people at the party. Not that it's out of the norm, but I always feel unsure of myself around him. It would be nice to have my best friend as a buffer between me and my dad's world. Namely, his growly, pissed off, and hot-as-hell teammate.

I force myself to relocate to the kitchen so I can grab a glass of spiced wine. I'm not going to listen in on what River's saying because that would be pathetic. Even though I blush and giggle in his presence, I still retain enough composure not to throw myself at his feet.

As I fill a glass with spiced wine, Devon and Damien are called into the living room by their beautiful girlfriends, Mila and Harper.

"You have to settle this debate," Mila says.

Harper's laughter is uncontrollable.

Devon and Damien look half intrigued and half scared as they pull themselves away from the ribs.

"I didn't think you'd be here," River comments, leaning

against the kitchen island. He studies me as I take a sip of the spiced wine.

I blush at his words. Does he think I don't have a social life outside of my dad's? "My dad made me come," I admit, smacking my lips together. "And Jasmine's working today so our apartment is quiet."

"Ouch." He places a hand over his heart. "You don't want to hang with the Bolts?"

I shrug.

He smirks. "With me?"

I blush harder this time. I know River recognizes it because his eyes soften the tiniest bit. They're nearly as dark as mine but significantly harder, edged in a steel I don't possess.

He tilts his head and shows me some mercy. "When do you fly out?"

"Tomorrow night."

He nods, takes a swig of his beer. "You staying in Seattle for the entire break?"

"No. I'll be back in time for New Year's."

River narrows his eyes, silently asking why.

"My sorority is having a huge New Year's mixer with this frat so…"

"I forgot you're in a sorority."

I duck my head, glance down at my plain T-shirt and jeans. "Yeah."

"I didn't mean—"

"Jasmine made me rush," I admit. When I meet his gaze, he's staring at me intently, a little line forming between his brows. "It's been good for me. There's only six other women in my computer science program so…" I trail off again. My palms tingle and I hold my glass tighter. Take another sip.

Why am I so nervous around River? Why does he keep talking to me when our conversations are always these awkward, confusing exchanges?

"They're lucky to have you," he replies, his tone serious.

I shift back, surprised by the certainty in his voice. "I don't really offer much."

"I'm sure you bring up the entire sorority's GPA." He chuckles lightly. "Hell, all of Greek life."

I grin. He has me there. "That must be why they keep me around."

He shakes his head and grips the back of his neck. Then, his eyes cut to mine again. They're dark and unreadable, two deep pools of black. "That's not why, Lola."

I draw an inhale at the intensity in his gaze. At the sound of my name on his lips. Before I can ask what he means, he changes the subject again. "You have a lot of friends in Seattle?"

"Yeah." I smile, thinking of my childhood and high-school friends. "It will be nice to see them. The whole group is coming home for Christmas so, I'm looking forward to it."

"A lot of parties?"

"Some."

"Old boyfriends?" His tone is teasing but his eyes still hold mine with a watchfulness that makes my blood rush to the surface.

I clear my throat. I think of the two guys I dated in high school. They were both quiet, respectful, nice guys. They were nothing like River, with his tattooed knuckles and raspy voice. "They're still part of my friend group."

He nods, as if I've confirmed something for him. His jaw tightens, not unlike Dad's when I piss him off.

"What about you?" I blurt out, wanting to shift the attention away from myself.

"What about me?" River mutters.

"Are you seeing someone?" I wince the second I say it because, desperate much?

"Several someones," he admits.

He doesn't say anything I don't know and yet, his words

cut. I look away again, not wanting him to witness the hurt that flashes through my eyes. I clear my throat. "Why not bring someone?" I lift my chin toward the living room, where my dad and Maisy are surrounded by their friends.

Harper is holding Maisy's left hand and by the way Mila is gushing, I know they're discussing wedding plans.

"Because none of them matter."

I look at River again. My breath freezes in my throat. I wish I understood half the riddles he speaks. I can never tell if he's being serious or teasing me, the same way the fraternity brothers like to mess around.

"So you just come and are forced to hang out with me?" I summarize. "By default, since we're the only two unattached people at these things."

He shrugs. "I don't mind."

I finish my wine. "Me neither."

River smirks. "Don't kiss any ex-boyfriends over Christmas break." His tone is teasing, his eyes unfathomable.

I snort. "Whatever."

He passes me a dish and we both make plates to pick on.

"Patton! Stop hogging Lola," Damien calls out, waving me over.

"Yeah, Lola, I wanna hear about California," Devon tacks on.

My dad groans loudly and Maisy wraps an arm around his waist. It's no secret my dad would prefer I remain in Tennessee. But, for someone interested in computer science and software development, Silicon Valley holds an allure that Knoxville doesn't offer.

I give River a small smile before I join the group in the living room. As I'm swept up in conversation, the afternoon slips away. Soon, the team is leaving, and I realize I won't see River again until after the holidays.

I wish I knew more about his holiday plans. Does his family have a big gathering, with grandparents and cousins?

Even though I usually exchange conversation with River at these events, I know almost nothing about him.

He's hardly forthcoming with his past or personal life and while I regularly stalk the shit out of his social media profiles, he doesn't post often enough for me to deduce anything with certainty.

"I'm heading out." River hugs Maisy goodbye. "Thanks for having me, Mais."

"Of course. Pass by over the holidays. Axe and I will be here."

"Yeah," he agrees, noncommittally.

Even though it's the lamest thing I've ever done, I scurry into the kitchen and pull out the tin of Christmas cookies I made River. I've already given tins to the Bolts women. It doesn't feel right to exclude him just because he doesn't have a significant other.

Or has too many.

Whatever.

I swallow back my nervousness and wait until Dad is saying goodbye to Beau Turner and his girlfriend, Celine, before I slip outside.

"River!" I call.

He's nearly to his car but he pauses when I say his name. Slowly, he turns toward me.

"Where's your coat?" he scolds.

I shiver against the cold wind as I approach him, holding out the tin.

"What's this?" His eyebrows knit together.

"I, they're cookies. Christmas cookies," I stammer.

He frowns. "You made them?"

I nod.

His eyes pin me in place. "For me?"

"I, yeah. Yes."

A devastating sadness sweeps River's expression for one heartbeat before his jawline tightens. "You shouldn't have."

"I hope you enjoy them," I forge ahead.

He dips his head.

I turn back toward the house.

"Lola." He reaches out and grasps my arm.

I freeze, his touch hot on my skin. He drops his hold and immediately, I miss his touch.

"Thank you," River's voice is gruff, underlined with emotion he rarely shows.

I smile. "Merry Christmas, River."

He scoffs, looking at the ground before meeting my gaze again. "Have a safe trip home."

"See you in the new year," I say.

"Get inside before you get sick."

Grinning, I scurry inside and close the door behind me. When I do, Dad looks over, his brows drawing together in confusion.

Maisy sighs, her expression knowing while Celine tosses me a wink. I roll my lips together to keep from laughing.

River Patton may have a long list of someones but I know he won't throw out the cookies I baked. I bet he eats every single one.

The thought warms me up more than the two glasses of spiced wine I nervously consumed.

ALSO BY GINA AZZI

Knoxville Coyotes Football:

Faked and Fumbled

Surprised and Sacked

Trapped and Tackled

The Burnt Clovers Trilogy:

Rebellious Rockstar

Resentful Rockstar

Restless Rockstar

Tennessee Thunderbolts:

Hot Shot's Mistake

Brawler's Weakness

Rookie's Regret

Playboy's Reward

Hero's Risk

Bad Boy's Downfall

Lock 'Em Down

Boston Hawks Hockey:

The Sweet Talker

The Risk Taker

The Faker

The Rule Maker

The Defender

The Heart Chaser

The Trailblazer

The Hustler

The Score Keeper

Second Chance Chicago Series:

Broken Lies

Twisted Truths

Saving My Soul

Healing My Heart

The Kane Brothers Series:

Rescuing Broken (Jax's Story)

Recovering Beauty (Carter's Story)

Reclaiming Brave (Denver's Story)

My Christmas Wish

(A Kane Family Christmas

+ *One Last Chance* FREE prequel)

Finding Love in Scotland Series:

My Christmas Wish

(A Kane Family Christmas

+ *One Last Chance* FREE prequel)

One Last Chance (Daisy and Finn)

This Time Around (Aaron and Everly)

One Great Love

The College Pact Series:

The Last First Game (Lila's Story)

Kiss Me Goodnight in Rome (Mia's Story)

All the While (Maura's Story)

Me + You (Emma's Story)

Standalone